THE TROUBLE
WITH WORDS

THE TROUBLE WITH WORDS

Chris Crowcroft

A Third Case for Richard Palmer, Investigator

AESOP Modern
Oxford

AESOP Modern
An imprint of AESOP Publications
Martin Noble Editorial / AESOP
28 Abberbury Road, Oxford OX4 4ES, UK
www.aesopbooks.com

First edition published by AESOP Publications
Copyright (c) 2017 Chris Crowcroft

A catalogue record of this book is
available from the British Library.

First edition 2017

ISBN: 978-1-910301-42-5

Printed and bound in Great Britain by
Lightning Source UK Ltd,
Chapter House, Pitfield, Kiln Farm,
Milton Keynes MK11 3LW

For those who wanted to see Richard Palmer
on the case again

Note: dates used obey the modern calendar not the old, when the year changed after March 25th.

Chris Crowcroft
chris@crowcroft.co.uk

~ 1 ~

'SO THIS censorship racket, how does it work?'

While he waited for his answer, Richard Palmer took the time to look his guest over as the landlord of the Bell Inn set two pots of beer down in front of them.

What he saw was a Whitehall type used to a life buried under heaps of scrolls and ledgers in the warren where Government operated next to Westminster Abbey. A solitary type, there was no wife and family at home in whichever cubbyhole this man occupied in the Palace of Whitehall. His religion was not to be enquired into either. In other times he might have been a monk.

The official remained silent, waiting for the landlord to leave them alone together.

Palmer knew what the man did. He was the trusted official of the Chief Minister, Robert Cecil, just made Earl of Salisbury for services rendered to the new Stuart regime. Palmer had expectations – he had formerly helped, as Cecil's go-to man whenever the playhouses and politics collided. William Shakespeare, in trouble during the Essex rebellion, and Ben Jonson on the fringes of the Gunpowder plot, were scores to the investigator's credit in this new century. A visit from Cecil's man must mean business.

At University in Cambridge, Cecil and Palmer had been contemporaries. Today they sat at opposite ends of the social pole inside the world of King James, the First of England these four years despite a series of plots to unseat him. That the plots had come from the religious right and left were signs of the unpredictable times.

'It's not for me to say,' the Whitehall man at last began to say, watching the landlord retreat, a pale smile around thin lips. 'It's a *complicated* business.'

It usually was, Palmer reflected who was pondering the Chief Minister's offer to put him into the censor's office. He would have preferred one of those perks paying good money for nil work done but then, as he told himself, his sort were condemned to work their arses off in life!

He took a long swig of beer.

'You've seen the Master of the Revels at work,' the official said.

Palmer had.

Edmund Tilney was a courtier of the old school, from the time of the late Queen Elizabeth. He handled the plays and players appearing at Court. He had also grown his influence to control all public performances in London, for example at the Globe Theatre on Bankside, over the Thames. In his time, thirty years and counting, the players had moved from life on the road to settlement in the capital following the money, and the power and the glory.

From what Palmer knew, the Master's hand plied the censorship tiller depending on the politics of the moment. Hard or soft, he made sure that nothing unfortunate went up in front of King James and his Danish Queen, Anne.

'Court taste is more sophisticated and tolerates riskier scripts than we permit on the public stage,' the official said, wincing as he tasted the beer, 'but eternal vigilance is all.'

Palmer didn't doubt it. When it came to hanging onto royal favour and the rich pickings that came from it, vigilance had feathered Tilney's nest for a generation and more.

'You know who will succeed Tilney?' the Whitehall man asked.

Sir George Buc, Palmer reminded himself, an altogether smoother sort as the dropped final k suggested. He'd purchased the right to succeed the current Master a decade back under the old Queen. It was no surprise in an age when everything had its price including options on the future.

'... and that there's no love lost between them?'

Well, there wouldn't be, would there, with the younger man waiting for dead man's shoes!

So why was it that the Chief Minister, in the mouth of the old official in front of him, wanted him to work for Tilney when Tilney was the outgoing man? Palmer didn't believe the nonsense he'd been told about 'learning from the old to help the new'. He didn't imagine that Tilney and Buc did either, especially old Tilney – he was bound to want to hang on to his lucrative position for as long as possible. They preferred to die in office, these old boys.

No, as far as Palmer was concerned, Robert Cecil, Earl of Salisbury, head of King James's Government as he had been of the old Queen's – he and his father before him – he never did anything for nothing, never had. One day his ask would come.

'So how are they going to work together?' Palmer asked.

'Buc has found an area which Tilney does not cover.'

'And what is that?'

'Checking plays put out for publication once they are finished in the playhouse. Tilney has never really touched the book trade – his heart's not in it. No, he likes to hear the plays read out, to give written directions where necessary – *guidance* he calls it – and to confirm it with the actors, but only in respect of performances onstage.'

'So Buc prefers to go by the book.'

The official managed a weary smile at Palmer's joke.

As for Tilney, everyone knew he made money from both sides, from the performers paying licensing fees and from the

Crown which retained him. Nevertheless the old fox had to be careful. What played all right today might turn out to be poisonous tomorrow...

... example, the Richard play.

Palmer called it back to mind. Mixed up in his first case for the Chief Minister, *The Life and Death of Richard the Second* had been used, in the time of the old Queen, to get the mob in the mood for regicide. It was what Sir Walter Ralegh, himself under lock and key these days, might call a hot potato. Its author, William Shakespeare, had barely escaped by the skin of his teeth.

He heard the official's voice go on, smoothly, reasonably.

'There's been a surge in plays being published.'

... now that one of the acting companies had transformed itself into the King's Men, glueing itself to the new regime. Hadn't the Scottish play come out of the last trouble Palmer was involved in, the Gunpowder treason? From strolling players to royal grooms in Lincoln green – the world had certainly moved on.

'I suppose Mr Shakespeare has his finger in this publishing pie?'

Palmer had form with the man, a King's Man today despite his shaky past. But there was one thing Palmer couldn't get. If the plays were so meretricious – and there was no doubt they were what with their flagrant breaches of all the classical principles – who on earth would want to buy them once they had outlived the stage? He could understand the popular fascination with spectacle – bread and circuses came to mind – but the educated reading public?

'Who can fathom public taste these days?' the Whitehall man said, venturing a second, suspicious sip of the brew in front of him. 'Buc certainly believes he has identified a niche where he can make his mark, and money too, from licensing fees.'

'Did nobody check the plays to be published before?'

From the expression on the official's face, Palmer knew that he was in for another of those explanations beginning with...

'It's a *complicated* business. There is a certain amount of regulation. The plays do have to be registered with the Stationers' company,' the official began to explain, referring to the guild which ran the printing trade from its hall nearby. 'The actors would be foolish to sell a play that was not the text agreed with Tilney, and the Bishop's censor has a last say on all books anyway. In times past, the City Government tried to involve itself as well...'

... which was one of the reasons, Palmer knew, that risk of political interference why the actors made sure they stayed outside the City jurisdiction, across the river. Bankside was a liberty, a free zone subject, from the mists of time to the control of another bishop, Winchester's. Its pimps, whores, hucksters and swaggerers and roaring boys, its vendors and traders, nips and other cutpurses, the players and the playhouse crowds, they all, one way and another, paid tribute into the pockets of the right reverend divine.

'Who is the Bishop of London's man?' Palmer asked, about the book censor.

'A ... er ... connection of mine.'

Palmer presumed he was another of these monkish sorts like the man in front of him. Old King Henry might have closed the monasteries but it didn't mean that the type had vanished. No, they just popped up elsewhere in the woodwork of State, like this one here in front of him.

'All in all,' the official concluded, 'there are gaps in our supervision and a need to bring the whole system – how can I put it? – into the seventeenth century. Buc will address himself to this task as he gains standing.'

So Buc, the coming man, had plans for change. Palmer's natural cussedness made him sympathise with old, declining Tilney.

'There's another piece of information you might like,' the official said, 'about the King's Men.'

'Oh yes?'

Palmer's whiskers were twitching, thinking of their chief writer, the Stratford man.

'They have a new plan in the making.'

'And what's that?'

'They want to go into the Blackfriars as well.'

The Blackfriars playhouse, Palmer assumed, on London's north bank. They already ran the Globe, a money-spinning amphitheatre under the open sky on Bankside as well as their lucrative appearances at Court in winter, touring old stamping grounds in the country in between.

Blackfriars would be a smart move into a smart location, a private, indoor theatre protected from the elements, available in winter when the Globe was unworkable and where the audience would be of the better sort, prepared to pay more. Palmer had learned a lot in the six years he had involved himself in the uncongenial business of plays and players.

'They hold the head lease after all,' the official said. 'Ten years ago, it was only local residents petitioning against them that kept them out.'

Including the man Shakespeare's publisher Field, Palmer recalled. Publishing the man was one thing, living cheek by jowl with him and his sort, evidently quite another. William Shakespeare might think the same too, if it happened at home in Warwickshire. Palmer had seen the actor's grand house and his newly respectable family close to.

'No chance of objections succeeding now, not now they are The *King's* Men,' he suggested.

'No indeed,' the official agreed with him, leaving the rest of his beer untouched.

After the Whitehall man had gone, Palmer finished up his beer while he looked through the file left with him. He smiled – a rare sight – at the official's parting words.

'No freelancing now, Mr Palmer. If you're to be a Revels officer it will take up all of your time.'

Palmer opened the file in front of him.

What he read detained him only briefly – records of a few poxy publishers.

Richard Field now – one-time Stratford friend and neighbour of William Shakespeare. He was the actor's first publisher until he'd signed that petition against playhouses in his neighbourhood in Blackfriars. According to the file, Field was keeping his nose clean and getting on, a big man in the publishing guild these days, in the Stationers' company.

Other publishers on file – Ned Blount, William Jaggard, Thomas Thorpe – were noted down for publishing the likes of Shakespeare and Ben Jonson, troublesome names known to Palmer from past casework, and Kit Marlowe, whoever he was. A couple of stray comments written in the margin caught Palmer's attention – Blount had a Jesuit brother, Thorpe had spent time in Madrid in the house of a well-known Jesuit agitator...

Oh the Jesuit connection! That old Catholic undercurrent still pumping dozens of underground priests into the country, to minister to the Catholic faithful, they claimed; to overturn King and State, so said the Government. A bit of both in Palmer's estimation; one Jesuit to his knowledge had ridden out to meet the Gunpowder plotters, another had done his inadequate best to stop them. It was the second who had swung for it.

Palmer took another swig of beer. Jesuits, Madrid ... Spain. Spain was the power most usually involved when it came to undermining the English State. It remained the evil empire, England's intending nemesis and chief enforcer of the Papal directive to remove Protestant monarchy and faith in England, by force if necessary. So it had been for as long as Palmer could remember.

But now the two nations were at peace – the Chief Minister's greatest achievement in the eyes of some, his greatest sin in the eyes of as many others. And all the while, Jesuit priests continued to ply their secret craft despite recent disruption, disruption Palmer had contributed to during the Gunpowder business.

It never ended, this old business, Palmer reflected as he finished his beer. His own Catholic family background complicated the picture further despite his own unbelief, helping burrow him in and among those Catholic insurgents, the ones he'd brought to book a couple of years ago – 'Remember, remember the fifth of November'. They had gone the way of the rope and the blade leaving their families to face ruin.

The memories disquieted him, in his dreams and now here in the comforting warmth of the Bell Inn. Yes, perhaps the quieter life of the censor's office would be better for him.

There was an autumnal snap in the air as Palmer walked the few yards from his lodgings in Cowcross Street to St John's Gate to meet Edmund Tilney in his office of the Revels.

The cold took the edge off the usual stink, from the river behind him which acted as an open sewer for human excreta mixed with the carcasses of cats and dogs, animal hides ejected from the local tanneries and other rotting flesh not excluding the occasional human corpse. Smoke from wood and coal did something but not enough to disguise it. It did nothing, either, to overcome the noise of men and beasts going about their business of the day.

The one-time Priory of the Order of St John was an impressive pile put to new uses since old King Harry Six-Wives had confiscated it from the hospitaller knights of the old faith. Palmer had walked up to it many times without ever having reason to go inside. Reporting in to the gatehouse he was led north past its old church, stone-robbed by a grandee to build his own Thameside palace before losing his head, or so Palmer's escort told him, until they found the rooms where Tilney held court.

The man himself appeared to be well into his sixties. Dressed to impress in a Court fashion ostentatiously rich in colours – blue, yellow and green – and made from expensive fabrics – satin, lace, taffeta and velvet – Tilney's outfit must have cost more than he himself earned in a year, Palmer calculated.

The old courtier was clearly not the sort who pulled his own pants on in the morning. Nor would his shirts smell of being washed in the filthy river. Palmer had his laundered in spring water pumped into the Charterhouse next door. He too was fastidious, if not outwardly so.

Tilney was ignoring him.

Ruffs were out and collars turned down, Palmer noted from the dress of the man in front of him. He found it odd when old men barbered their hair in the latest style in contrast to their sagging, mottled faces to which Tilney's was no exception. Palmer went in for shabby Elizabethan.

Tilney finally looked up. Palmer sensed himself being surveyed with disapproval.

'It's nothing personal, Palmer, but I don't want you.'

Palmer was not surprised, he was ready for it.

His appointment was not in the gift of the man in front of him, it belonged to Tilney's boss, one of the great ministers of State. What the Lord Chamberlain might agree with the Chief Minister trumped any independence of Tilney's. Theirs was a pond bigger than the one Tilney lurked in, like some old carp hugging the muddy depths here in his Clerkenwell pond.

Palmer tactfully did not say it; it was enough that he knew, and that Tilney knew that he knew.

'What would you say your qualifications are for the post?'

Tilney's question was not friendly.

Since when were qualifications necessary to get your snout in the gravy train?

'Doing what Lord Salisbury asks me to,' Palmer said, dropping the name of his patron, the Chief Minister.

'So I've got no choice,' Tilney growled.

Palmer changed the subject.

'Your rooms, sir, they are very impressive.'

'Yes, I continue to do my duty here, whatever Buc may think...'

Tilney's shot across the bow deliberately singled out his contracted successor.

'... I shan't be retiring to Leatherhead, not just yet.'

So he had his own mansion in the country, Palmer guessed – one of those men on the make, made up over the last generation.

Tilney was a long-time Howard connection, Palmer already knew, a family which managed to prosper despite its Catholic faith. The current Howard chief, responsible for the King's security was the same Lord Chamberlain who was requiring Tilney to take Palmer on.

But the status quo couldn't last forever. The Chief Minister's official had conceded one last piece of information: Tilney was ill and had money troubles – they all did, these people, even the Chief Minister, Palmer reminded himself. Public office was an expensive business. Salisbury was up to his eyes in debt for keeping up with his royal master in the necessary style. It was the price paid for a successful life at Court. If you were lucky, it fell to your heirs to pay it.

Palmer spoke up.

'What can I do to help?' he asked Tilney.

The older man growled again.

'Christmas.'

Was that it, Christmas? Palmer waited to be enlightened.

'... it comes early for us. We settle our plans in November; well, I *say* that – the old Queen never wanted plays until Christmas but Their Scottish Majesties desire them to be ready from Hallowmass so you can see what we're up against!'

Hallowmass was at the start of November. Palmer counted himself among those who were not thinking of Christmas in November even if the Court was.

'What is happening this year?'

'A normal Christmas, thank God! But even if the first play is on St Stephen's, the night after Christmas, we go on to the eve of Lent. It means we still have over fifty nights of entertainment to provide – comedies, histories, tragedies, bear-baiting, tilts and jousts – double that if they call for the early start at Hallowmass.'

'Masques?' Palmer asked, trying to appear knowledgeable.

He'd seen a fashionable one by Ben Jonson and Inigo Jones. His buttocks ached at the memory.

Tilney's reply was contemptuous.

'That's the job of the Master of Ceremonies.'

No love lost there, Palmer noted. Did everyone at Court hate everyone else? Silly question!

'I create a list of the plays to be considered,' the old Master went on, 'starting with some of the older ones Their Majesties haven't yet seen.'

... from the time of the old Queen, Palmer guessed, when the Stuarts were immured in their Scottish fastness. How long had Elizabeth been gone? Four years, coming up five in the spring, he calculated. Palmer was surprised he was still here. Plenty weren't.

'... and I bear in mind that the three royal children are showing an interest in the plays. So I add some of the newest and latest.'

'Who by?' Palmer asked.

'From the King's Men mainly but not entirely. Under Elizabeth, licences were restricted to two companies, two only being authorised to appear in London – there have always been plenty of others out on the road. Now we have *four* as each of the royal children gets their own company, selected on *my* advice. As you can imagine, all of these agitate to appear at Court at Christmas, all must be accommodated, in the order which *I* decide.'

Even so, the King's Men – Shakespeare, Burbage, Hemmings and the rest – they held the prime position was what the old courtier was saying. Good close season business for them too, Palmer reckoned, even better if they were to run the Blackfriars playhouse as well.

'Yes, Her Majesty will want to see her own Men, Worcester's as were, and there is also Prince Henry's company to consider.'

.... the old Lord Admiral's before they were re-assigned to the strapping heir to the Throne. Keep up, Palmer admonished himself.

'Anything from Ben Jonson?' he speculated.

'Not since last year. He's more involved in the *masques*.'

Masques were unwelcome words in the Tilney vocabulary and outside his jurisdiction.

'Masques are a licence to burn money. They cost four times as much as a play brought in by one of the licensed companies. It's all this wretched new passion for *scenery*, and stage *machinery*. A little of Inigo Jones and his designs does not go far, not in money terms let me tell you!'

Palmer tried a little deference.

'May I ask, sir, what practical form the business takes?'

Tilney's clothes appeared to inflate as he prepared to expatiate.

'We tell the acting companies which plays we want in case there's any reason they can't revive them. We check their playbooks to see what guidance we gave first time round – dull job, so it'll be yours – to ensure there's no reason for me to withdraw my original signature of authorisation.'

Palmer knew what he meant. He remembered the Richard play with its scene of the deposition of an anointed monarch and the trouble it had caused in the wrong hands at the wrong time.

'Readings before me I restrict to new plays,' Tilney added.

'And when is that?'

'Usually in the spring. And let me tell you this, Palmer, we're talking of each company producing a dozen and more new plays each year so this is not light work – fifty plays plus in total, every one to be carefully checked. I hope you understand that.'

Palmer gritted his teeth. The Chief Minister's old official had not been lying. This censoring was a full-time job, real work of the sort Palmer liked least, paperwork.

'As it happens, I am a little light-handed,' Tilney admitted. 'I have put one of my best men into sorting out those wretched children's companies.'

Palmer knew something about them, the Paul's Boys connected with the Cathedral and protected by the present Queen who liked their infant sauciness. Palmer was grateful that he was to have nothing to do with these nests of little vipers.

He heard Tilney sigh long and theatrically.

'All right, Palmer, if I must take you, these are my rules.'

His suit inflated for a second time, straining buttons, eyes and hooks.

'You may be called on to be my deputy so you turn up clean and punctual, and for Court appearances, *smart*,' he said, casting a withering look at Palmer's threadbare suit. 'Respect the actors – the playhouse proprietors too for that matter – but no hobnobbing, and no bribes; that's what they pay licensing fees for and they pay them to *me*.'

Palmer nodded his understanding.

'Steer clear of the masqueing, jousting crews – any trouble with them, and you refer it to me. Same goes for the children's companies. Last of all, *never*, *ever* let one name cross your lips.'

Which was, Palmer asked with humble eyes?

'Buc!'

'I do so much hope that we shall be able to collaborate happily.'

The man Buc, opposite, was altogether a different sort from Tilney, fond for a start of a Latin word where an English one would do.

Palmer was sitting across town in a small room in the Palace of Whitehall to keep this second appointment arranged for him by the Chief Minister's official.

Sir George Buc, minus the original final k, was visibly a man of the new order. He dressed in sober black and white suited to the younger breed of professional politicians led by the Chief Minister himself – the togati, as they liked to be known, wearers of the metaphorical senatorial mantle rather than those bearers of arms, the peacock military faction at Court. The togati had taken on and beaten the soldier sorts like Lords Essex and Southampton in the time of the old Queen. This situation persisted under James. Politics was now a game of the mind rather than the strong right arm. Policy trumped chivalry.

Palmer put Buc in his forties, a former envoy abroad clever enough to get himself knighted by King James, at extra cost. In one sense Buc was lucky in his purchase of the next mastership after Tilney. Some men were buying up reversions on reversions, having to wait out two lives such was the Scottish monarch's canny skills in finding new ways of lining the royal purse.

If only the King didn't immediately overspend what he brought in! Despite his allegiance to the more sensible wing of the regime, Buc had served with Essex in his Spanish campaigns, the old official had made sure to tell Palmer, bringing the news of Elizabeth's last and disastrous favourite's triumph back to London.

What was out was now in, Palmer reflected, on how times had changed under King James.

Lord Essex had ended up dead and a dirty word after his last ditch rebellion against Elizabeth. Yet now Essex's son and heir was back in favour – Palmer had endured the Court masque to celebrate his marriage into a loyalist family. As for Essex's co-plotter Southampton, he was lording it high in Stuart favour after his own spell in the Tower. Going the other way? Ralegh, Captain of the old Queen's Guard, in the Tower in his place.

And here in front of him sat ambitious Buc. Palmer shifted the conversation on.

'I hear you will license the plays for publication, sir, when and if they go into print.'

'It needs to be done. Wouldn't you agree?'

Palmer thought Buc's question over.

'Not something Mr Tilney has done much of.'

'Just so. The world moves on. Does one exist if one is not in print?'

Palmer was not sure he agreed – folk got into trouble when they wrote things down was his experience. A large sheaf of private sonnets by the unlikely poet from Warwickshire came back to mind – he still had them somewhere.

'But what is written needs to be measured,' Buc added, his voice staying within its even tenor, 'weighed in the balance.'

'My understanding is that Mr Tilney continues to authorise the plays for...'

Palmer faltered in finding the correct, diplomatic formula. Buc helped him out.

'... for as long as he wishes and has the health and skill to do so. In the meantime, I look to the new ground, licensing plays in print which, to be frank, the clerical authorities have little taste for or experience *in* for that matter. It would help,' he said, giving Palmer a frank look, 'if I had sight of any restrictions already put on the texts, if Mr Tilney permits.'

Or even if he doesn't, Buc left unsaid, and that he would look to Palmer to help him with it.

'Do you know the acting companies well, sir?' Palmer asked.

'I *think* I can say that I have that side of the business in hand,' Buc smiled. 'I acquired the reversion some years ago.'

He was just the sort to get on with them too, Palmer thought, this lover of plays however fantastic they might be, carrying the spectator all over the place, out of time and form entirely against all classical rules. Better not get started on that...

'However, the printers and publishers,' Buc said, 'they are more of a closed book to me.'

Palmer dutifully laughed. So that was it, he had his orders – to help the new man with Tilney and to do his dirty work among the printers and publishers.

He expected to be sent away with this understanding. Instead Buc detained him.

'What is your interest in politics, Mr Palmer?'

None if he could help it, beyond keeping an eye out for what affected his own interests.

'We live in new times,' Buc began to say, not interested in any answer Palmer might give. 'His Majesty...'

Yes, it was 'Majesty' these days, imported from Scotland. The smaller the country, the bigger the title. The old Queen had been happy with 'Highness,' her father with 'Grace.' Whatever next?

'… has united four realms, in spirit if not by constitution.'

Formal union had been ruled out by Parliament. King James was disappointed, so disappointed that he was not keen to call any other assembly unwilling to get the answer right, for *years* if the rumours were right. All the same he'd had himself styled in consolation King of Great Britain and his image stamped on a new unpopular coin, a pound of fiscal persuasion called the Unite.

'He has settled, as near as anyone can, the dissension between the radical and the conservative elements in the Church.'

Palmer knew just what Buc meant. No bishops, no kings! James had threatened the Puritan zealots while refusing to punish Catholics as a class for the aberrancies of the Gunpowder plotters. All the same, the Government had put up the fines for recusancy, for those of any faith who refused to conform by attending church under the new rite.

Palmer knew all about it. It was how the Palmer estate in Kent had perished by the recusancy of his stiff-necked father, speaking out for the old faith in the old Queen's time.

Buc brought him back into the present.

'There *is* peace with Spain, Mr Palmer.'

But apart from peace, the desire for union and a settled religion…

'The times are changing, Mr Palmer. There is a daily line for us to tread – on blasphemy, on the presentation of monarchs and other important figures on the stage and in politics of course. At the same time, our scope is greatly enlarged. With the King passionate in debate and much published himself, it will be bound to rub off into our not so little world.'

For a second time Palmer assumed that the interview was over. He made to go but Buc held onto him.

'Has Mr Tilney heard about the latest gem being polished up by the King's Men?'

'You mean the playhouse in the Blackfriars?'

Buc shook his head.

'No, not that, interesting though it is and a sign, shall we say, of the improving times. No, I'm talking about their new spectacular – *Pericles.*'

'Father of the Athenian state?'

'No, *Pericles Prince of Tyre.* A romantic story – wife lost at sea, miraculously rescued and rediscovered years later. Or so one hears.'

Palmer groaned inside.

'Mr Shakespeare's latest?' he guessed. 'Is it a matter for us? Isn't it something for Tilney, a play not a book?'

'You're right of course ... but there's talk of one George Wilkins writing it – not a name I know enough about. I like us to keep our ears close to the ground, thinking forwardly...'

... and of his succession, sooner or later to Tilney.

Palmer was relieved to be back on firmer ground. Wilkins was a common enough name – there was a publican of that name with premises on the corner of his street in Clerkenwell.

'You may want to look into him,' Buc said, rising from his chair to indicate that their meeting was finally over.

T HE TAVERN on the crossing of Cowcross and Turnmill
streets was no more salubrious than when Palmer last
remembered it. It was the kind of place where you hid
your money safe inside your clothing before you
entered. Its light was poor, not helped by the black-stained
woodwork, its atmosphere redolent of stale beer mixed with
wood and unswept, unclean sawdust. There was only one
reason to patronise it, which was what went on upstairs.

His eyes quickly accustomed themselves to the dark and
found the landlord.

'How's Kath?' Palmer greeted him, asking about his wife.

'Big and fat, same as always,' the landlord replied.

There was no humour or affection in the remark – George
Wilkins was a queer one, no doubt about it, Palmer thought
who was used to all sorts.

'The usual is it?' Wilkins asked him, signalling to his
tapster to pour and deliver.

Silence followed. Palmer sipped his beer carefully in case it
was off. If it was, there were ways to tell this landlord and ways
not to, not unless you wanted trouble.

'I've got a new pair of girls,' Wilkins said. 'Dark, say
they've got Italian blood. That's what you like far as I recall.'

Was it, Palmer asked himself?

There had been one in his youth – dark, yes, father Italian.
She'd cropped up not so many years ago right at the heart of
his first case for the Chief Minister. Where was Emilia now?
Last seen in the company of a pious noblewoman living in the
country and having religious visions. It seemed to him to be a

strange reversal of outlook, from impropriety to piety. Yet plenty of folk had taken the same path.

Not Palmer...

He said something idle to his host who did not respond – he was not the hospitable sort.

'Apparently you have a namesake who fancies himself as a writer,' Palmer tried again.

Palmer saw a dangerous look in Wilkins's eyes. So it *was* him. He judged it unwise to say anything about his own translation into the censorship office.

'Well, I always took you for an educated man, George,' he said instead.

'That's just as well, Richard.'

Silence.

'My father was a poet...' Wilkins started to say, watching Palmer with a careful eye for any sign of disrespect.

Palmer put on his interested look.

'... I tried my hand at it early, but there wasn't much money in it...'

Wilkins's eyes appeared to shift, darting around the room.

'... until last year, when I thought I'd have another go.'

'I heard it was to do with *plays*,' Palmer said.

'Like as not.'

Palmer waited. Wilkins's eyes went on dancing.

'*The Miseries of Enforced Marriage* was what my play was called,' Wilkins said, looking over in the direction of his wife who was serving food to a table of customers over by the door. 'That's what it was about – did well, well enough to be published,' he said, as if he couldn't have cared one way or the other. 'Led to others...'

'With the King's Men was what I heard,' Palmer prompted him.

'You'd be right. There's another one on the go, for the same company...'

Pericles, Prince of Tyre, Palmer wanted to say but held it back which was just as well when he heard what Wilkins next had to say.

'... but I'm not at liberty to say. Can't be too careful. Ideas are easy stolen,' he said, turning his full gaze on his questioner.

Palmer deflected it.

'The King's Men – isn't the man Shakespeare their chief writer?'

'Mebbe.'

Palmer held back, waiting for more. Wilkins was not disposed to be helpful.

'What's it to do with you, Richard? I know your business, running after the young wives of crusty old aldermen. Why are you asking so many questions?'

Palmer made something up about needing to keep track of the man Shakespeare, old business to do with unpaid bills.

'We all have those,' Wilkins said, a second reason for him not to help his customer.

He walked towards the door.

'Lodges round here or used to, Master Shakespeare,' he turned back to say, 'Silver Street, by St Giles's Gate, round the corner from me. Haven't seen him since the lady of the house died.'

Palmer remembered the place from that first case, when the writer went to ground with a Huguenot family – it did him no good, Palmer had found him all the same. The lady of the house? He remembered a woman, not old, not young, with a heavy *Frr*ench accent.

'Does he...?'

Palmer left the question incomplete, his eyes indicating upstairs.

Wilkins shrugged neither yes nor no.

'Oi!'

A loud voice of protest interrupted them, exploding from over the other side of the room where Mrs Wilkins was serving.

'.... we're not payin' good money for this *tripe*!'

Wilkins looked across but said nothing.

Palmer watched him gnaw at a straw as if in thought. Then Wilkins strode towards the troublemaker – a punk, a whore, out with a customer she had picked up in nearby Smithfield with its fairs and executions and all manner of entertainments. Her punter looked to Palmer like a country boy, like enough a cattle herder, and drunk.

Her complaints grew louder as Wilkins approached, turning to screams of fear.

Without warning, the landlord kicked the stool from under her and sent her sprawling in the sawdust. When her punter lurched upwards to remonstrate, Wilkins dealt him a backhand smash which sent him reeling towards the door. The cowering woman's eyes showed fear of the landlord's knee which was drawn back to strike her. She slithered away in the direction of the door, taking the punter with her, his hand held to a bleeding mouth.

Wilkins came back to Palmer as if nothing had happened.

'If you're interested, let me know,' he said, nodding towards upstairs.

Palmer trudged up the creaking stairs. Another customer, staggering down them towards him barged into him as he went by. He let him pass. Unlike Wilkins, Palmer had no appetite for a fight. He was in his forty-fourth year, he reminded himself, he was getting on, slowing down.

The smell of the place began to change, from stale beer on wood to the odour of cheap scent over bodily odours of a different kind. He reached the top the stairs a little out of breath. He looked around him. There was a small fire in the hearth opposite. Otherwise the room, which ran the length of the building, was divided into a series of cubicles screened by dirty curtains hanging from rafter to floor. A woman's laughter, coarse and encouraging, was giving counterpoint to rhythmic male grunting.

By the hearth, a young woman had her back to him. From the way she was tidying around, she was the skivvy, Palmer decided, and occasional stand-in if business was brisk. There was one thing about her which struck him, the pale red colour of her hair.

'Take a stool while you wait, sir, and what'll you drink?'

The familiar country accent brought back a memory, of a hot day by the river in Oxford and a girl in the water...

The red-haired girl turned to face him.

'Ellen?' Palmer asked.

Palmer saw the expression on her face, guilt followed by defiance.

'What are you doing here?' he demanded.

'Might ask the same o' yow.'

'Where's the child?'

... the baby girl which he had delivered from a rescued girl and brought back to life in the cold river water. A bloody miracle, he'd said, so Miracle, Ellen had called her and had him stand godparent.

'Where she's always been.'

With the couple who ran the tavern in Oxford where he'd taken mother and newborn child, with the Davenants.

'They loves her like their own. She 'as money for when she's grown.'

His money, Palmer knew, gold angels from his work for the Chief Minister. He didn't resent it. It stood in place of himself, it provided better than ever he could.

He moved towards the hearth, taking a stool.

'So what happened?' he asked, waiting for another version of the old, old story.

'Got bored,' Ellen said as if that was reason enough, 'the work was 'ard.'

They both ignored the drumming sounds of a bed, wood on wood, coupled with the noise of brute male climax.

'This man came by, one of them play actors, took a fancy to me, said 'e'd take me away to see London, an' 'e did 'til 'e fell sick, then this other woman came in for 'im – mother of his bastard child, she said. Well, she could 'ave 'im, I said.'

There was no sympathy in her voice, just a sing-song story getting another run out.

'So I looks for work such as I know, and all I knows is tavern work.'

It made Palmer feel old and cold.

As for the child Miracle, Ellen was right, she'd be all right, the Davenants would look after her, there was money, she needn't turn out like her mother here in front of him. He would go and see the child, now that he was settled in a regular job, once the Court season was over. Meantime he'd send her something at New Year.

'What was the name of this actor?' he asked.

Ellen appeared reluctant.

'Don't want to get 'im in no trouble,' she said; 'not 'is fault 'e's sick.'

His look insisted on an answer.

'Shakespeare,' she said at last, then seeing the surprised look on Palmer's face, added, quickly, 'no, not that one, 'is brother, Ned as I calls 'im.'

Edmund, Palmer mentally corrected her, his mind going back to a performance before an angry, ageing Queen which had helped save Edmund's brother William's life.

The noise behind the curtains subsided. A man stumbled out, doing up his belt. Ellen nodded in the direction of the vacant berth. Palmer shook his head.

'So, this is what you want?' Palmer asked her.

Ellen pouted like the young woman she was, not yet twenty Palmer calculated, digging into the recesses of his memory, more like eighteen.

'What else is there?' she asked.

What could he do for her? He warned himself off – even the Good Samaritan had not taken the victim into his own house and bed. Would the Davenants take her back? Maybe, on account of the child. But would she stick?

'The work's not 'ard 'ere, I gets tips,' Ellen said.

And the rest, Palmer thought to himself. And what was to come? More babies, disease and then the street.

'If I give you some money, do you get to keep it?' he asked her.

'As I said, I gets tips,' she replied.

Palmer delved into the depths of his doublet to find his protected money. He pulled out a couple of bright silver shillings and watched Ellen's eyes light up. It was what she valued above all else, he reminded himself as he handed them over. Why should she be any different? He had hoped the Davenants might change her, them or her baby Miracle, a better bet – but they had come too late.

He was going to tell her where he lived, in case she was in trouble but he stopped himself. He knew what would happen –

trouble – and that she would come, sooner or later. Life had made her what she was, and him too. He was not the saviour of the world.

He got up to go.

'I'll keep an eye on Miracle,' he said, feeling the need to offer her something.

'Yow won't be stayin'?' she said, nodding towards the curtains.

Palmer shook his head.

At the bottom of the stairs, he came across Wilkins.

'Suit you?' the landlord asked him, barely masked contempt in his eyes.

A thought crossed Palmer's mind.

'The country girl up there,' he said, 'worth looking after.'

Perhaps it would help for Wilkins to know that someone was interested in her.

The flames from two large candles threw a flickering light around Palmer's tenement chamber. Very little had changed in the years he had rented it. What had it accumulated?

Nothing much, other than dust. True, he could afford candles these days and seacoals for a fire in the small hearth. Once, not so long ago, he had deserted it for gentleman's lodgings until another attack of plague had driven him back to where he belonged, here.

There in the centre of the room sat his ark, the one remaining Palmer heirloom, his bed. Whatever else was in the room qualified as no more than landlord's sticks – a gimcrack chest and a three-legged stool. There was a cracked pitcher for water and a rough earthenware bowl for night use. The cloth which used to cover it had disappeared a long time ago. The room stank every time he came back in, a stink more than just his own, a smell deeply pitted into every fibre of a building neighbour to a stinking sewer of a river. The Fleet? More like the Sluggard, its oily black waters blocked by the waste deposited into it every hour of every day and night.

Laid out on the bed was a new suit of clothes, plain black material, a white soft-collared shirt and fresh hose, quality wool Palmer sensed as he ran his hands over the material. Tomorrow was his first day in the new job – a salaried officer of the Revels!

He felt as nervous as on all those other nights before – when he'd left home for university in Cambridge and later for the inns of court in London to study Law. There was the night before he left for the continent to soldier in the Low Countries in the Protestant cause (thank God his Catholic father was dead by then).

Thoughts of another night in this bed pricked his loins, the night with Emilia, arid, past reason hunted, once had, past reason hated...

Where were those sonnets?

He leaned down to trigger another secret from the bed, a hidden compartment. There was little in it. Such money as he had these days was lodged with a goldsmith off Cheapside. There was his sickness discharge from the Army in case the authorities tried to press him back into service; he was too old anyhow.

Taking up most the space was what he was looking for, a thick wad of papers in an unbound manuscript – sonnets, one hundred and fifty of them give or take, confiscated from their author six, nearly seven years ago.

He pulled out a specimen from the middle of the pile and took it to the nearest candle.

Or I shall live your epitaph to make,
Or you survive when I in earth am rotten.

Not true, not true in either case, of poet or muse. The writer was now a King's Man with a big house in his home town bought from the proceeds of his trade – Palmer had been there, he had seen it. The young man the sonnets addressed? An ornament at the Court rescued from his spectacular disgrace but past his best, no longer 'fresh' or 'green'. So these days it was Mr Shakespeare, Gentleman and Groom to His Majesty, looking up to the Right Honourable the Earl of Southampton, Master of the Queen's Horse. They were no longer the figures of romance they had believed themselves to be. Yet both looked down on him.

What might the sonnets be worth?

Palmer weighed the goods in his mind – author, the favourite playwright of the people; his muse, back as a favourite at Court. Subject, love – a dangerous one, dangerous to them both, dangerous to Palmer too if he opened this Pandora's box.

Even after all this time?

The acting companies picked up only a few pounds for their cast off plays sent for publication, enough to keep a man for a year, or so he'd learned sniffing around the clerk in the Revels office after his interview with Tilney. He'd lived on less in his time.

With such provenance wouldn't these sonnets do better?

He'd have to act quickly, where was the harm, wasn't it what everyone did? Wasn't the Chief Minister himself rumoured to be taking money from the Spaniards as a mark of his role in brokering the peace with them? Emilia's husband, fat, pink-faced Lanier of the broken nose – the nose he, Palmer had broken for him – wasn't he on the take as well with his Government perk?

The whole world was at it.

A draught fluttered the corner of the sheet of paper he was holding tight in front of him.

Palmer put it back under the bed. It was not yet time.

~ 3 ~

'YOUR ATTENTION please, *gentlemen* – as some of you might think you are!'

Tilney's joke, not new, provoked dutiful laughter from the small crowd of actors in front of him. Plenty of them had invested in gentility right down to a coat of arms designed by the ever-flexible heralds to show how far they had risen in the world. They were men with London addresses, wives and families, country origins long since forgotten, with one exception.

'The King's Men first – what d'you have for me? Mr Shakespeare? Shakespeare? Wherefore art thou, Shakespeare?'

More laughter.

'Not present, Master!'

Palmer recognised the booming voice. It belonged to John Hemmings, a man he'd run across before, a senior man in the King's acting company.

'He's been down in the country, for the wedding of his eldest daughter to a doctor and a gentleman.'

Palmer's ears perked up. Well, well. His mind went back six years to the awkward young Puritan Dr Hall and more kindly to the bride – Susanna, wasn't that her name?

Hemmings was telling only half the story. He was holding back worse – that this absence limited what Shakespeare had ready to offer for the coming Christmas season. His friend's was the author's name the Court looked for. Rumours that their chief writer was finished could be the only consequence. Their competitors here today would gleefully spread them.

'We should like to offer *Anthony & Cleopatra*,' he put in quickly, before the other companies could take advantage.

'Ah yes,' Tilney recalled who had authorised it only months earlier. It had done well or so he'd heard. 'A classical subject, from Plutarch, I fancy,' he said looking around for approval.

Hemmings fawned a smile. He cleared his throat.

'A tale of eastern empire and sensuality,' he announced, 'overcome by Roman virtue.'

Didn't King James see himself as the modern Augustus?

'Yes, that will do, on the face of it,' Tilney said. 'We'll take another look at the text. There have been no changes in performance since I signed the text?'

'Nothing important,' Hemmings said. 'We've cut it here and there of course.'

'… for which His Majesty will no doubt thank you!' Tilney said, to more laughs.

King James liked the drama, but only up to a point. Hunting pleased him more.

'Now what else is there?'

Hemmings appeared stuck.

'In terms of Mr Shakespeare's plays, nothing *completed*. There's work in progress of course.'

'Of course,' Tilney said, begging the answer.

Hemmings came closer to, keen that what he had to say should not be heard by others.

'A Greek subject, to do with one Timon of Athens,' he whispered, 'and another one, about the Roman hero Coriolanus – both from Plutarch. Mr Shakespeare is working on them as we speak.'

Privately, Hemmings wasn't so sure about *Timon*; it was sitting around incomplete despite or because they had assigned the main responsibility to a younger writer, Thomas Middleton to lead a collaboration on it. William appeared more interested in co-writing these days. Was he flagging?

'Working in the country, is he?' Tilney said, eyebrow raised, leaving no doubt where he thought Shakespeare should be, here in London, here for him, the Master of the Revels, today.

Hemmings nodded.

'And that is it?'

'What about *Pericles*?'

It was Palmer who spoke up.

'*Pericles*?' Hemmings asked, annoyed at the revelation.

'*Pericles, Prince of Tyre.*'

Hemmings was in a quandary. Truth was his company had seen a few early scenes but they had their doubts. The writer, Wilkins was relatively untried, his ideas for how it would work out were, frankly, disturbing...

'Mr Palmer has just joined the office of the Revels,' Tilney interposed, '*my* office.'

Hemmings knew who Palmer was – a troublesome informer for the Chief Minister during the awkward Essex affair, awkward for the actors because of the abuse of their *Richard* play, perceived to be *their* abuse until they had made excuses acceptable to the authorities.

What was Palmer doing here now? It worried Hemmings. He liked to give Palmer and his sort a very wide berth indeed.

'Work in progress, Master, work in progress,' he started to explain, 'and not in fact by Mr Shakespeare.'

'Not by Shakespeare? Then why are we talking about it?'

Hemmings could not resist a wicked look in Palmer's direction. Palmer mimed a bow in return.

'We need something for Her Majesty's tastes,' Tilney said.

It was Queen Anne who really liked the plays and her taste was for love and romance.

Romeo & Juliet was proposed, a play which it surprised everyone to hear Their Majesties had never seen. It was more than ten years old. There was a lot they hadn't seen in frigid Edinburgh before their arrival in the English capital. This was giving the acting company's playstore a new lease of life as well as taking some pressure off the Court's insatiable appetite for new work.

The meeting broke up on that positive note.

'I hear the younger Shakespeare's sick,' Palmer said to Hemmings. 'Is your man William sick too, in the country, in the care of his new doctor son-in-law?'

'No.'

'Young Edmund, not been concentrating on the job?'

Hemmings snorted in response. Edmund Shakespeare – Ned to his friends and all the women who chased after him – he had never been the reliable sort; not that he was going to say that to the man in front of him.

'We expect Mr *William* Shakespeare back any day,' he said.

Tilney was not best pleased once he had Palmer to himself.

'Too forward, Palmer,' he said, referring to his intervention over the *Pericles* play. 'I prefer my people to speak *to* me when they're spoken to *by* me.'

Palmer was experienced in official reprimands. They were like water off a duck's back.

'Right!' Tilney said, pushing a manuscript across the table, 'that's the Egyptian play for you. Check it out for any previous instructions by me.'

'And the *Romeo & Juliet*' Palmer asked. 'Has its age created anything to worry about?'

It was a fair thought. Tilney chewed it over.

'Tragic love story as I recall, not much in the way of politics beyond a pair of quarrelling families and a foolish old friar. Come to think of it,' he said, a gleam in his eyes. 'His Majesty will no doubt find a useful moral in it. He likes to be seen as a peacemaker. Now let me see, he will most likely *opine* that he would never have let the – what were the families called? oh, never mind – he would never have let them go so far in their hostility to each other. Peacemaker you see. I heard him use the word just the other day, to young Robbie Carr...'

Carr was not a name Palmer knew and showed it.

Could he trust his new assistant? Bit of a rough diamond, Tilney reckoned, but then he'd known the father – old man Palmer had come from his part of Kent. Some of the Palmer confiscated land had come his, Tilney's, way.

'Robert Carr,' he explained, 'young, Scottish, blond, a groom of the royal bedchamber.'

He gave Palmer a knowing look.

'Carr broke his leg in a tilt – last March it was. His Majesty *nursed* him personally. Certain people are predicting great things for young Mr Carr. Others are not so happy about him. These are matters you need to know,' Tilney put in hastily as if to justify his liking for a good gossip.

'Who might not be happy?' Palmer asked.

Pretty well anyone who resented the Scots influence at Court.

'Lord Pembroke for a start,' Tilney said.

The chief of the powerful Herbert family, Palmer knew full well, a young man hitherto prepared to play the public if not the private part of King's favourite. Bold enough to step out of line when first presented to the King and kiss him on the face. Favour had followed. Had it been returned?

Whether it had or not, it was clear that this Carr was the new favourite.

'We see a lot of Pembroke,' Tilney said, 'and he likes the plays, actors, writers – there isn't one who hasn't dedicated something to him, looking to his generosity.'

Yes, now that Lord Southampton was past his flower of youth and beauty, Pembroke had become quite the patron of the arts. He was no beauty but he was young and without the burden of a wife. So where did he stand given the arrival of Robbie Carr?

Warning entered Tilney's voice.

'Listen, Palmer, I knew your father, well enough to wish well to the son. He lacked only one thing, a conscience sufficiently *supple* for the age. I hope that I shall not be obliged to say the same about you.'

Palmer touched his nose. Conscience was no such burden to him.

~ 4 ~

THE MUD-STAINED traveller looked around the room in the Bankside alehouse.

'Good God, it's Will! You're a sight for sore eyes,' John Hemmings said as soon as he saw him.

William Shakespeare pulled up a stool by the fire. Hemmings signalled to the landlord for a pot of beer. He waited. Shakespeare did not speak.

'Where are you lodging?' Hemmings asked.

A tapster arrived with the beer. Shakespeare left it untouched and the question unanswered.

'Have you been writing?' Hemmings asked him more anxiously.

It was the pressing need, from all their points of view.

'Tilney has been asking.'

Shakespeare shrugged.

'You got the news about Edmund?'

This had more effect on the arrival.

'Where is he?'

'Not far from here, in a room – I've made sure it's clean and warm. He's not well, not well at all.'

Both men knew what that meant.

'How long has he got?' Shakespeare asked.

Hemmings spread his hands.

'Only God knows, the doctor cannot say.'

The two men fell into an awkward silence.

'How was the wedding?' Hemmings asked.

'He's a good man, Dr Hall,' Shakespeare conceded after some time.

Not good enough to do his new father-in-law much good, Hemmings reckoned to himself. He'd hoped that rest, country air and some herbal purging would have set his colleague on the mend. There was nothing better than the dropping of a batch of turds to make a man feel better about the world, was his opinion. Yet the malaise of the last few months seemed no better than it had been before for the man in front of him. Was it of the body or of the mind?

'There's a child on the way,' Shakespeare said, as a matter of unremarkable fact.

'Great news! You are to be a grandfather.'

'Where is he?' Shakespeare asked, meaning his brother.

Hemmings told him.

Without another word, Shakespeare stood up to go.

He found his brother stretched out in bed. The wracking cough he heard on the way in and his brother's emaciated appearance confirmed to him what was wrong. It was the lungs. Of all things for an actor, the lungs.

Edmund Shakespeare gasped a greeting. The worry in his eyes belied a joke on his lips.

Shakespeare put out his hand to find his brother's. He found it feeble and cold. The boy was dying, twenty-seven and dying while he was forty-four and fully intending to live. He remembered when Edmund was born, his mother's last, when he himself was already a young man, and how he had been delighted to play father to him in the crowded family home on Henley Street; less delighted when he became a father for real and the house became a prison.

'Susanna,' he said, smiling, 'sends her love.'

It was enough to convey all his daughter had said to him to tell her favourite Edmund. She was only three years younger. They had been as brother and sister.

A wracking spasm turned Edmund's face away.

'Mother too,' Shakespeare added.

He hadn't told her how things were going with her youngest although she must have guessed what with his brother's absence from the wedding. She was old herself and failing. Not that he would tell Edmund that. Their mother would hold on for the birth of her first great-grandchild – it was what lay uppermost in her mind. He prayed that Edmund might outlast her and spare him having to tell her the news. Every son is a coward in front of his mother when it comes to bad news, he reflected.

He looked around him. So here it was, the end, in a paltry backroom. What was there to show for it? No wife, despite a bastard boy dead and buried. A brief name on the stage and a painful, early exit. Nothing uncommon in that, Shakespeare reflected even if he had so far outwitted it himself. Faces from the past flashed past in his mind's eye, too many for the pageant to end. Was it his fault, taking the boy off to London just after he himself had lost his only son? Where had the plan gone wrong, the one anointing Edmund his heir?

He looked back to the invalid in the bed.

Edmund was sleeping, innocence returned to his ghastly white face. Suddenly Shakespeare was overcome with tiredness. There was a couch nearby. It looked like a stage property borrowed and installed by Hemmings for whoever might be watching over the sick man. From the Egyptian play, Shakespeare guessed.

He stretched himself out on it. Before he had time to pull his boots off, he was asleep.

'Coriolanus – Roman hero of the early Republic, I found him in Plutarch.'

Shakespeare felt better after a night's rest and for being back where he belonged as he set to, explaining the outline of his new work to the senior men in the company.

He looked around them – Hemmings who liked to be thought of as his discoverer twenty years ago; the Burbage brothers, the one his leading man, the other the Globe's man of business; Condell, a churchwarden in his respectable private life; Armin who played the fool, musical, subtle (which could never be said of his predecessor Kemp who'd played the crowd at the expense of the play); veteran Will Sly kept on for old times' sake.

'Victor over the Volscians…'

'Over the who?'

The voice was Hemmings's.

'Doesn't matter, John – enemies of Rome. Our Coriolanus is put up for consul.'

'So where's his weakness?' Burbage put in, guessing that the part was his.

'Pride. It goes against his nature to ask the people for their approval.'

'Not like us, then!' Burbage said, sharing the joke among his colleagues.

'But he does it. The stumbling block is a row over the corn dole to the masses.'

'Very topical, Will. There's a lot of protest going on about corn prices.'

The voice was Armin's.

'So, where's the action in all this political stuff?' Burbage asked.

'At the beginning, when Coriolanus wins his glory and his name in battle – from the conquered city of Corioli, for the pedants among us,' Shakespeare said, smiling at Condell. 'After that, when he is rejected by the Roman people and sent into exile.'

'What happens then?' Condell asked, who always wanted the detail in everything – scripts, accounts, actors recruited to the company.

'When he joins his enemies to march on Rome. And these enemies are, John?'

'The, er, Volscians I assume. *Everyone* knows *them*!'

'Yes, I can see it,' Burbage said over the laughter, imagining big, meaty speeches for himself.

Shakespeare saw the wistful look. He gave him a taste.

Mend and charge home,
Or, by the fires of heaven, I'll leave the foe,
And make my wars on you.

Burbage mouthed the words silently after him, cocking his head in satisfaction. Will never let him down. No-one else had ever come near him, not in Burbage's self-interested opinion.

'Is it finished?' Condell butted in, asking the practical question.

'Half done,' Shakespeare admitted. 'I've roughed it out in full – there's an excellent scene where the mother of Coriolanus – stern matriarch sort – takes him to task for assaulting Rome....'

The few weeks spent in Stratford with his mother had reacquainted him with the type.

'... but there's a lot of prose still to be put into verse, scenes to be completed...'

'We need it and soon, Will,' said Hemmings. 'We're very short of new work – Tilney picked us up on it when he called all the companies in about the Court season. Turning up short-handed left a lot of scope – too much I say – for Prince Henry's Men, and the Queen's. What has happened to the *Timon* play?'

'I can't get it to work,' Shakespeare admitted. 'It's not mine anyway, it's Middleton's.'

Collaborations did not always work, he wanted to say about his ambitious co-author, but he held it back. It was he who recommended them. His time was shorter these days and he had thoughts of spending more time in the country. Collaboration kept his hand in when inspiration otherwise failed him. It had helped him in the beginning. He hoped it would help him towards his end.

'What happens to Coriolanus?' Burbage asked.

'*He* spares Rome, the Volscians kill *him*.'

'Another happy ending...'

Burbage's brother Cuthbert was the unhappy voice.

'... to add to all those others of late – a black man's jealousy, the murder of a king's favourite daughter, misery in the Scotch mist...'

'All of them very powerful, Cuthbert,' Hemmings admonished him, 'and more to the point, *successful*.'

'That's all very well,' Cuthbert Burbage answered back, 'but is that where the public taste is leading us?'

'We lead, brother, we don't follow.'

The voice was his brother Richard's.

'Yes, well, I know I'm the businessman, but look around us. What have we had from Jonson since *Volpone*? Nothing! He and Inigo Jones are too busy with their masques for the Court, and what's at the heart of them? Music, dancing, *spectacle*. Look, we've said as much before; whenever we take on the Blackfriars – if the plague lets up and we ever do – it'll be time for something new – stage machinery, special effects. We have to move with the times!'

'I see,' Shakespeare said. 'You think I'm behind the times?'

There was an awkward silence and exchanges of guilty glances among the senior men until Robert Armin spoke up.

'What about *Pericles*?' he asked.

'It's hardly new,' Shakespeare protested, 'it goes back to limping old Gower, if you're game for tumpety-tump in rhyming couplets...'

Gower was to be found, flat on his back in gaudy, painted effigy in nearby St Saviour's church. The text Shakespeare had so far seen had about as much life.

'... what next, Chaucer?'

'You chose it, Will,' said Armin, wounded.

Hemmings quickly intervened.

'To meet Cuthbert's point, from what Wilkins has shown me, it has a tremendous range – scenes in, where was it? Tyre, Ephesus, Tarsus, Antiochus, I think – no *Volscians*, however.'

The joke relaxed the little gathering.

'We could do a lot with that,' Cuthbert Burbage said, 'but I'm only the businessman.'

'I'm not stopping you,' Shakespeare said. 'I've always accepted that we stage work by other writers and I've found most of them for you. So, if you want *Pericles*, by all means do it.'

'There's one problem,' Hemmings said. 'It's not very good, at least not what Wilkins has shown me so far. In the writing, that is. The ideas behind it are a marvel.'

'What's the problem with it?' Richard Burbage asked.

'Where does one start – we have Gower the poet as Chorus…'

'Chorus worked well in *Harry Five*,' Sly said, who liked to hark back to the past.

'That's as may be,' Hemmings agreed, 'but Wilkins has gone overboard for the antique style – "iwis", "y-slaked", "y-ravished" – and I can't for the life of me persuade him out of it. We could have done with you here Will, we really could.'

'Just needs a good bookman,' Sly suggested, a play doctor.

Wasn't that how Will had started in the first place after all?

'There's more,' Hemmings said. 'As you know, Pericles loses his wife in a tempest at sea. In the case of the royal princess, Marina…'

'Beautiful name,' Shakespeare admitted.

He had only himself to blame for Wilkins's writing ambitions, from when he'd lodged in Silver Street in the north of the city. His landlords the Mountjoys, they'd had a pretty daughter, there was an apprentice they wanted married to her – the mother did anyhow – and a dowry to be settled. How had he allowed himself to get mixed up as a go-between in family business?

Sure enough, there was a falling out, sending the young folk round the corner to live with… George Wilkins. A man on the make, that was how he remembered him on first acquaintance, wanting to chance his hand in the playhouse and insistent about it too. Marie, that was the name of the mother, Mary the girl. Marina, now that *was* a beautiful name…

'She ends up in a brothel,' he said to his colleagues.

Wilkins knew all about brothels, he kept one of his own, known to several of the men present.

'I can't see Tilney liking that!' Armin said. 'King James has a daughter.'

'Provides a point of sympathy?' Shakespeare suggested. 'Her shining virtue keeps her pure, that sort of thing?'

'There Wilkins parts company with us,' Hemmings told them. 'That's not the story he wants to tell. He wants to tell it... how it is.'

'Well, he'd know all about brothel life,' Sly said, only to feel put out when nobody laughed, especially those who knew Wilkins's tavern first hand.

'Let me guess,' said Shakespeare, 'he has her defiled, but redeemed. Is this where the goddess comes in, Diana, to restore her chastity?'

'Just so,' Hemmings said.

'It'll never work,' Richard Burbage said. 'Tilney won't have it, audiences aren't ready for it. What's his excuse?'

'There's the rub. Wilkins points out that in *Lear*, our own Mr Shakespeare departed from the old play to have the favourite daughter Cordelia killed. Quite right, he says, it's the dramatic truth of the situation. He goes on a lot about it – dramatic truth – this Wilkins does, I can tell you.'

'Is he not prepared to change his script?' Cuthbert Burbage asked.

'No.'

'But are we all agreed, or most of us,' Burbage said looking at Shakespeare, 'that the story has promise?'

There was a murmur of agreement.

'Then what he needs is a *collaborator*!'

All eyes turned on Shakespeare.

'Am I dying?'

Edmund's voice was feeble.

'Doesn't sound like it to me,' his brother lied.

Edmund began to cough. He wiped the blood-fleck phlegm from his mouth with a filthy rag. He examined the caked linen with curiosity.

'I know what this means,' he said.

'I've brought some excellent remedies with me, from our Dr Hall,' Shakespeare said, anxious to improve the mood of the patient. 'Try it – it's a compound you have to smoke,' he said, handing over the pipe already lit.

'What's in it?'

'Aniseed, honey, egg, dried and powdered, filled out with tobacco. He says he's had great success with it.'

Edmund inhaled with suspicion, putting the pipe aside after a couple of attempts.

'Tell me about the wedding,' he said.

'It was a wedding,' was all his brother would say.

Edmund laughed, a painful, cracked sound.

'So you let her go, at long last.'

Shakespeare was nettled – what did he mean? Susanna was twenty-four – the women in their family didn't marry young by and large – the groom was thirty-two. It had been a principle of the Doctor's that he could not marry until he was thirty and with a successful practice. He had not come courting, sensible man, until both thresholds were crossed.

And not before time.

Susanna had been turning headstrong. Take her refusal to take communion at Easter last, it had put her into the sight of the authorities for recusancy. Failing to attend church spelled the risk of heavy fines, fines for a father to pay opening up a road to ruin for more than just the offender. Puritan Dr Hall's religion had brought a positive influence to bear on his new wife's behaviour.

'How was mother?' Edmund asked.

'Pleased – a doctor and a gentleman for her grand-daughter's husband. Dr Hall looked after father at the end, remember, to mother's approval.'

'Doctor … gentleman. Means nothing to you, of course.'

The painful, cracked laugh repeated itself.

'How is your wife, how is Anne?'

Ah, Anne.

'A wedding pleases a mother as much as a bride,' he said.

Her eyes had laughed and cried like he hadn't seen in years, on a fine June day among family and friends in the great church where the knot was solemnly tied and afterwards feasted, danced and drunk – very, very drunk – in the big house at New Place; all without undue haste, unlike their own, his and Anne's.

'Did I say Susanna is expecting a child?' Shakespeare said. '*After* the wedding night,' he added to leave no doubt that everything had been done properly, in the right order, between Susanna Shakespeare and Dr John Hall. It had not been the same between him and Anne.

A well-endowed child it would be, by her grandfather's fortune and her father's lucrative practice. Please God the child would be safely delivered, and safely grow and if so, what could then go wrong, if Susanna behaved sensibly? The family was set to prosper. It hadn't always been so for the Shakespeares, by no means.

'You're to be a great-uncle,' he added.

'Are you … writing?' Edmund summoned his strength to ask.

When wasn't he, Shakespeare was tempted to say. Except that the last months had been difficult. *Coriolanus* wasn't coming easily, this man of rigid pride and honour with his distaste for the easily-bought plebeians. It was all there to be described – the entire panoply of human frailty on every side. But he was tired of it, tired of all roads leading to failure. If the hero was heroic in his falling, the crowd loved it – that the great could suffer too made up for the trials they faced in their own little lives.

But he knew that failure could be base too. He had tried saying that in his Trojan play. It had not gone down well. Perhaps that was what his colleagues had been trying to say, the fear that they, *he* was repeating himself. How many times had he reshaped himself? Did he have it in him to change yet again?

'Another of your battlers ... against the walls ... of fate,' his brother gasped. A ... a good part in it ... for me?'

Shakespeare could have wept.

'It's a play without any romance or humour,' he said.

'There is humour in everything ... even in this,' Edmund said, referring to his condition.

Shakespeare kept the tears at bay. Was he beyond feeling? Had he seen and done too much?

'I've got a mind to do something with Alcibiades – the golden boy of the Athenian Greeks.'

It was his latest thought on how to rescue the *Timon* play, by inserting a notorious troublemaker from ancient history to give the story a broader span.

'He's much more your type!'

Edmund appeared to digest the suggestion before changing the subject.

'Where ... are you staying?'

'I'm staying here, until you're better. I can work in that little penthouse in the Globe.'

'Staying here?' Edmund wheezed. 'I *must* be dying.'

~ 5 ~

I T WAS A TIME of learning for Palmer.

The manuscript entrusted to him, of *Anthony & Cleopatra* was licensed under Tilney's signature which he found at the back. It was otherwise unmarked.

He had made the mistake of suggesting some alterations.

Tilney bristled.

'You are not a criticaster...'

A weird species of playhouse hanger-on. Palmer had met one once, who called himself a critic for short, at a masque in the Banqueting House, Ben Jonson's masque.

'... or a play mender. Be very clear, Palmer – I say this for your own good – it's not your job. *Your* job,' he emphasised, stabbing a finger in Palmer's direction, 'is to use your judgement to prevent unfortunate words or thoughts reaching fine ears or provoking the worst sort of reaction in the teeming populace. It is a *political* skill, not an inventive one. Christ knows, we have enough fertile minds as it is without adding another one in the Revels office!'

Palmer looked suitably chastised.

'There is a simple job I ought to be able to trust you with,' Tilney said, mollified in part by the show of contrition.

He pushed over a square notebook. Palmer opened it. It was an account book, he could see but written up in childishly bold, unformed handwriting in shiny black ink. Its columns listed the acting company booked, the name of the entertainment, dates and payments. *The Moor of Venis*, the first entry read. Not a great speller, Palmer reckoned, even by the standards of the day. Obviously a play, and by the King's Men too. Christmas season 1604. He racked his brains.

'I like to get the actors to use a secondary title which reminds me what it's about,' Tilney said.

When Palmer still didn't get it, Tilney lost patience.

'It's called *Othello*, for God's sake!'

Oh yes, Palmer remembered, the black general tupping his white bride, along with a rival except he wasn't, and all a lot of bother over a handkerchief. He couldn't imagine old Seneca bothering with a thing as flimsy as a handkerchief.

What he most remembered was a minor character called Emilia, the villain's wife and a waiting woman; which was what Mrs Emilia Lanier was these days, wasn't she, away in the country with the Countess of Cumberland, whatever else she liked to think?

Tilney brought him back to the present.

'Look at how I do it and do the next one the same way!'

Palmer made himself a regular at the hall of the Stationers' company where all books, plays included, were registered for publication. He familiarised himself with the more regular names – Heywood, Dekker, Rowley, Marston, and others, common or garden names as he expected them to be – fine gentlemen had no need to earn their living by scribbling despite rumours about the late, unlamented Earl of Oxford or the rising Francis Bacon. But then, Bacon was no fine gentleman, more like a poisonous snake in the grass from what Palmer had seen of him, busy in the courts, at Court, changing sides whenever it suited his ambitions.

He spotted a couple of titles associated with the novice Wilkins. He got to understand who the publishers and booksellers were and who printed for them and how the roles were sometimes exchangeable. Some names frequently repeated – among the publishers, Edward Blount who appeared to have a taste for Ben Jonson among others.

When a name from the Chief Minister's file cropped up – Thomas Thorpe tainted by Madrid and Jesuitism – it was the association with Ben Jonson which caught Palmer's eye. There was an entry by Thorpe for the arse-numbing masque Palmer had once seen, the marriage-extolling *Hymenaei* and a play, *Volpone*, both by Jonson. Thorpe's entry demonstrated that it was he who intended to publish.

Palmer invested a small bribe in a snout in the Stationers' office who agreed to send him private lists of plays registered, or likely, or rumoured to be. Among all the dross in the reports which came, he was to look out for the name of Shakespeare.

The Shakespeare list was already extensive. Recent publications – *Hamlet*, *The Merry Wives of Windsor* – took it past a dozen. *As You Like It* and *Troilus & Cressida* were both registered but not yet printed, the first with a notice of 'stay' on it.

What did that mean, Palmer asked?

'Most likely a protest from the owners of the original script who seek to stop publication,' the snout explained.

'The acting company?'

'They may think it's not yet played out. Or they disapprove of the version submitted which has been pirated...'

'Meaning?'

'A rogue publisher sends his spies in to memorise the text or pays an actor in the cast to do it for him. Publication in this way – or so the actors *say* – is a double bind. It spoils the play for the stage and its inaccuracy upsets the writer.'

'So the play is not owned by the writer?'

The snout gave Palmer a very sharp look – whatever could he be thinking of? Ownership of plays belonged to those who paid for them, the acting companies or the publishers they sold to.

Title belonging to the author? Whatever next!

The season brought in the smothering skies of November, its cold settling deep into the ground, its frosts unmelted by the rays of any distant sun.

Palmer received a notification from his snout about Shakespeare.

A pair of publishers were about to register the writer's *King Lear* for publication. Their names meant nothing to him but he took the news to Sir George Buc, what with his interest in licensing play publication.

'An excellent work, *Lear*,' the smooth ex-diplomat said. 'I saw it when it had its Court performance, last Christmas, St Stephen's night I believe. Have you read it?'

Palmer had, from Tilney's papers authorising it for public performance.

'What was your impression?' Buc asked.

Mindful of his mistakes with Tilney, Palmer opted for humour.

'Don't give your property away till after you're dead!'

It was a preoccupation of the times – old man wants looking after passes his property to heirs provided they move in and care for him. And what do they do? They force the old man out.

Lawyers were making plenty of money drawing up contracts to meet the situation, or so Palmer understood who had done more than one strong arm job for and against in his time.

Buc smiled.

'Myself, I took it for a unity play...'

Blasted unity, Palmer cursed inwardly, the King's single most treasured idea.

'... which our playwright chooses to demonstrate by the effect of *dis*unity created by the very character who should know better – the King – when he divides the country between his daughters.'

'In the original play,' Palmer offered, 'I've heard that the youngest daughter did not die.'

'Yes,' Buc agreed, 'but with Shakespeare there is no reprieve for her or for her father Lear. It is the natural consequence. Tell me, Palmer, which of the two do you believe?'

Palmer didn't answer immediately since he would have said 'neither'.

'I've learned not to act the critic, Sir George,' he said.

Buc laughed aloud.

'Which is why I sit here and you there.'

The evening's performance of the revived *Romeo & Juliet* in the Great Chamber of the Palace found Palmer in his place at the back of the room. Tilney was lording it up front with the royal party, King and Queen and royal children.

The last time Palmer was here had been among the actors on the other side of the divide. The same tapestries, of monstrous satyrs cavorting in sylvan glades, rippled on the walls caressed by candlelight and cosseted by the music of woodpipes and strings.

This time the room was full – it was a performance for pleasure and not for life or death as it had been with the *Richard* play acted out in front of stern Elizabeth. Death had touched her since, others too – the actor Phillips, happiest when playing his viol, absent from his place in the consort playing tonight at the side of the stage. Palmer saw him again in his mind's eye, sharp-faced, nervous.

He did not know the play but the story and some of its lines had become proverbial, even to resisting ears like his own.

He was interrupted by a door opening briskly onto the stage.

Two households, both alike in dignity,
In fair Verona where we lay our scene...

Palmer recognised the actor. It was Shakespeare, setting the scene. He was wearing a fine cloak and hat with an enormous feather meaning something or nothing.

From ancient grudge make to new mutiny,
Where civil blood makes civil hands unclean...
A pair of star-cross'd lovers take their life...

'So much for the suspense of the story!'

The voice, gruffly recognisable came from over Palmer's shoulder. He turned round to see Ben Jonson, so-called friend of Shakespeare, rival playwright and royal masque-maker who gave him an outrageous, provocative wink.

A clash of swords onstage called Palmer's attention back.

The crew onstage were rioting in gaudy, primary colours – scarlet red, azure blue and canary yellow, indications of what the Veronese wore however long ago. More like a reminder of the previous reign, Palmer sensed, which now seemed, in all its colour and glory, much longer in the past than the ten years since the play was first performed.

Is the day so young?

This must be Romeo.

'Oh dear, oh dear...'

Jonson's chuckle was unkind. The Romeo onstage – Burbage, stout and forty was not helped by a youthful wig perched on top of the solid figure beneath it. He was standing in – Mercutio was his normal part and that ten years ago. Both roles belonged to a younger man surely. The sick Ned Shakespeare? Where were the young men in the company?

I am not here. This is not Romeo.

'You're telling me,' Jonson whispered, a loud stage whisper.

Light laughter spread around him.

A party of women appeared on the stage, Juliet at the heart of them with not much to say except to respond dutifully to her mother's suggestion of marriage; a boy, from the fluting, treble voice, followed by a party of men in masquerade in their brilliant colours, Romeo among them, a Montague in disguise at the Capulet feast.

He bears himself like a portly gentleman.

'I'll say he does!'

Jonson again; Palmer's temper snapped.

'Out!' he growled, turning on the half-heckler, bustling him out of the chamber past the two Yeomen of the Guard on the door.

In the passage outside, Jonson looked his ejector up and down.

'So, what have we here – it's Palmer, Palmer of the Revels!'

The man was drunk.

'So there really is no honour among thieves.'

As he levelled the accusation, Palmer pushed Jonson up against a wall.

'Oh, *piss* off,' Jonson spat back. 'They get far worst at the Globe. We're not in church you know. It's a good play, I admit … when properly cast!'

'That's not for you to judge!'

'Or for you, rat's breath. I'd have expected better of Tilney, he's an old hand.'

'It's not up to him who is cast as what.'

'What! Tilney picks the play, he presents it at Court, he's responsible whether he likes it or not … and that means he's responsible for a Mercutio playing Romeo who'd be better off thinking about Friar Laurence these days. Just goes to show, Tilney's losing his touch. Thank God the new man is more *couth*!'

At the reference to Buc, Palmer slackened his grip.

'Tilney's here till he dies,' he told Jonson.

'And how long will that be? We both know Edmund Tilney's old and ill.'

'And so?'

Jonson guffawed.

'You don't apprehend me,' he said, 'you don't get it at all, do you?'

'Get what?'

'Buc comes in and then … someone else buys the right to succeed *him*.'

'And who would that someone be?'

Jonson's laugh rumbled up from the bottom of his jutting gut.

'Me, Mr Palmer. And when I come in, you can be sure that I will have no need for you. You will be out on your slimy, skittery arse!'

Enough! Palmer forced the man off the premises, watching him stagger unsteadily into the night.

He stayed outside in the frigid night air to think about what he had been told.

So, Jonson was ambitious, not only for money and fame but also for position. It was not what he'd said around the time of the Gunpowder plot when he was happy to act the great iconoclast, scourge of men and their morals. Maybe the one led to the other? But a poacher like him, would they really set him on to patrol the acting game? A bricklayer's stepson and a known brawler, advanced to Master of the Revels?

Palmer shook his head. It was a Court post suited to a man of credit. Times might have changed but they hadn't yet turned upside down. As for Jonson's threat to his own position, Tilney lived, Buc was still to come, so he, Palmer had time, years; and years meant money to one used to living from week to week.

He went back up to the Great Chamber where he persuaded the guards to let him back in by showing his badge of office. He was in time to see the closing tomb scene in the play – dead bodies everywhere. What would Aristotle have made of it?

At the end, as the players accepted the Court's polite applause, the King broke with all protocol and left his royal throne. Mounting the low stage, he united the hands of the bereaved Lords Capulet and Montague, heads of their warring families.

The applause exploded, louder than any the actors had received.

Ah, yes, Palmer thought, the great Unifier...

~ 6 ~

'**Y**OU DO *not* leave a room before the King!' Tilney shouted at Palmer in the morning.

Palmer shrugged.

'There was someone who needed removing,' he said.

'Which is *not* your job. It's a matter for the Commander of the Guard.'

Tilney gave Palmer a curious look from the corner of a puffy eye.

'Who was it?'

'Jonson, drunk, taking the piss.'

'Ah! Not for the first time.'

'Ben Jonson fancies himself for Master of the Revels one fine day.'

'Ha!'

It was as much as Tilney had to say on the subject.

A rare night off took Palmer back to Clerkenwell via the bridge over the river, and home. Before he reached his tenement he had to pass Wilkins's tavern. A girl sweeping out caught his eye – Ellen – and something else about her too.

'Are you well?' he called out.

The girl looked swollen. Was she ill?

'Wadda yow think,' she answered, carrying on with her job.

So that was it, Palmer told himself, guessing her condition. It hadn't been apparent when he'd last seen her, a couple of months before.

Behind her, Wilkins appeared in the doorway. He motioned her inside. He glowered in Palmer's direction.

'How's the writing going?' Palmer asked him.

Wilkins folded his arms.

'How's the job with Mr Tilney?' he asked back, distrust in his voice mixed with threat.

So he knew.

'It's a job.'

Which was true. The novelty, of splendid rooms peopled by the fashionable and the powerful, fine clothing, generous food and drink and sumptuous entertainment had worn off. Palmer was, he accepted, a servant. It was no more than a job.

'And the writing?' he persevered in asking.

The tightening of the landlord's folded arms said 'why should I tell you?'

'You'll see it soon enough ... in your line of work.'

Wilkins intended no friendliness as he stood aside to let Palmer enter his premises. Business was business after all.

The two men settled in silence, Palmer with a mug of beer, Wilkins without. When Ellen came by with her broom, Wilkins jerked his head to tell her to move off.

'As you can see, she's been plugged ... and sprouting,' Wilkins said dismissively.

Palmer kept his temper. He shrugged.

'Some men like 'em that way,' Wilkins said, a question to Palmer in his eyes. 'Others can't bear 'em, after childbirth. Me? I'll take what I can get so long as it's not *fat*.'

This he directed over his shoulder towards his wife working nearby.

Palmer brought the beer to his lips.

'What will you do with Ellen?' he asked.

'Get rid of her,' Wilkins said, 'but not yet, not while she's got work left in her.'

'Isn't it a hazard of the trade?' Palmer suggested. 'Do you get rid of every girl that breeds?'

'Mostly,' Wilkins said, sardonically amused. 'This one I told to go see the local hag who does the necessary but she wouldn't. As far I'm concerned, there's plenty where they come from, and their season is short before they're swiven out or poxed up.'

'And the girl?'

'Not the right commodity,' Wilkins said, like a judge of the flesh herded along the street outside to the meat market in Smithfield.

Palmer changed the subject.

'What about the writing?'

Wilkins returned his original dark look.

'Come to a halt,' was the answer Palmer got.

'Anything to be done about it?'

'Get Mr Shakespeare run out of town?'

Wilkins's suggestion was only half in joke.

'Here's how it is. Since Mr S has come back on the scene, I am told I do not give the King's Men satisfaction. What I *have* given them is the idea, and the first nine scenes.'

'What's the story?' Palmer asked.

Wilkins looked at him with suspicion.

'I'm not in the writing business,' Palmer reassured him. 'The business I *am* in is going to need to see it anyway.'

Wilkins grudgingly gave way.

'Pericles, Prince of Tyre ... he seeks the hand of the King of Antioch's beautiful daughter. He must answer a riddle. The answer contains a secret, that the king has unnatural relations with his daughter. If Pericles reveals it – death; if he fails to answer – death. With me so far?'

Palmer nodded.

'Pericles flees the country. In a tournament he wins a king's daughter. They marry, conceive a child, and are about to return to Tyre when ... and that's where we're presently becalmed, me and the King's Men. What *should* happen next is a shipwreck.'

'Not so lucky, this Pericles,' Palmer said, attempting to lighten the conversation.

Wilkins glowered at him for a second time. He picked up the story again.

'Thaisa – that's the princess – she appears to die in childbirth...'

'*Appears*,' Palmer picked up on.

'Appears ... and is put overboard ... but she is washed ashore alive at Ephesus. Pericles deposits the child – Marina – with the governor and his wife at Tarsus. She grows up into a great beauty, to the disadvantage of the governor's own daughter so his wife conspires in her murder, *except...*'

'... the cold-hearted murderer takes pity?' Palmer suggested.

'No, she's captured by pirates...'

Oh God, not the pirate routine.

'... who put her in a brothel...'

Try that for size.

'... where she is corrupted and rediscovered by chance, by Pericles.'

'You're not suggesting...' Palmer began to say.

'Yes, it mirrors the scene at the beginning.'

The implication of incest.

'No happy ending, then?'

'Oh, we deal with that in a final scene. Thaisa has become a priestess in the temple where Pericles and daughter go to expiate their sin. The goddess Diana appears – we'll use a strapping lad and the latest in stage machinery. The past is wiped away as if it was all in a dream.'

Absolution, Palmer told himself, and what a dangerous idea it was.

'So what's the problem?' he asked. 'The brothel scene?'

'That is just *one* of Mr Shakespeare's disagreements with me.'

'There are others?'

'Sure...'

'Rhyming couplets for Gower, the old tetrameter – interesting bu-u-t...'

But what? Wilkins's eyes had demanded, up in the little penthouse in the Globe theatre a few days earlier.

'A little old-fashioned, don't you think? And the brothel scene...'

Wilkins couldn't see why not, hadn't Shakespeare killed his own Cordelia?

The man had a point, Shakespeare conceded. Did it go a step too far, or did the problem run much deeper? He was a man with daughters of his own. Since they had arrived at marriageable age, was he less inclined to the lascivious, was that it?

He thought of his daughter Susanna, married and with child in the correct order of things. She was to stay in her father's house, the grandest house in Stratford bought to proclaim his restoration of the family name. Her husband was part of the household. They looked after his wife, Anne and the other daughter Judith while he was away. One day they would do so for him.

What should such a paterfamilias have to do with virgins broken in brothels?

It was not his only conundrum. He had laid aside the *Timon* play. His own contribution to it was in little more than sketch form. With the Roman play, *Coriolanus*, he was nearer to the end. It was an unloved child, his harshest yet, no less true for all that. Why was there no tenderness in it? A scene between mother and son gave scope for it, but no, in writing it down the scene demanded that it be about duty whatever else he tried to say.

Was there no tenderness left in *him*?

It was surely a time for redemption, not for the sort of squalor and degradation Wilkins was proposing however much it might reflect the truth.

'So, how's it been left?' Palmer asked Wilkins.

'Mr Shakespeare is to *collaborate* with me on the play.'

Meaning rob the writer of his idea and take the credit, Palmer read in the angry eyes of the man opposite. To redeem it was the last notion Wilkins would have believed.

'And will you do it?'

'Don't see why I should.'

Palmer got out into the open air with relief and turned for home nearby. He had hardly started when a figure flew out of the alleyway. It was Ellen.

'Yow gotta 'elp me,' she demanded.

Palmer took her back inside the alley, away from any eyes that watched.

'What can I do, Ellen?'

He could give her money to help her disappear. She would head for the street and soon be back for more. If the Davenants in Oxford could be persuaded to take her back, she wouldn't stick, the same if he found her a place somewhere else, and how likely was that for a pregnant girl? No, she'd had her chance.

'Take me 'ome!'

For a moment he thought she meant Oxford, until he realised – *his* home, the chamber in the rundown tenement up the street.

'No-no-no-no-no,' he objected.

'I can't stay 'ere, 'e'll kill me and the baby soon as not. Yow don't know what 'e's like.'

Palmer could guess, but to do what she asked would make him a target instead, a target just up the street. The situation was impossible.

'You'd rather he kill me instead?' he told her frankly.

'But 'e told me, something about yow bein' an ... officer o' the Crown.'

Whatever it meant, it was a head start on her in terms of protection.

'No!' Palmer repeated emphatically.

'So yow won't 'elp? I'll tell 'im ... I'll tell 'im yow ... tried to take me away!'

Palmer pulled her round to face him, hard enough so that she should be as frightened of him as she was of Wilkins.

'You be a good girl and get back in there. I'll try to find a way of getting you away safe.

~ 7 ~

'**I** AM THE RESURRECTION and the life...'
The great bell was tolling high above them in the tower of the church on Bankside, the one favoured by actors.

The priest intoned the opening words of the burial service as he met the corpse on its bier at the entry to the church. Scattered snowflakes floated down onto the mourning party. It was too cold for heavier snow, so cold that the stiff carcasses of a pair of tiny birds lay on the ground, deep-frozen on their perches even before they fell to the ground. The little corpses drew Shakespeare's eyes away from his dead brother. Men had walked across the frozen Thames that morning for the first time in living memory.

I know that my redeemer liveth.....

The language was quaint, older than he was.

We brought nothing into this world neither may we carry anything out of this world.

It was true enough, about Edmund. There was precious little left of him, of goods stored up or of his sad, wasted body.

Man that is born of woman hath but a short time to live and is full of misery.

How to tell his mother, that her youngest, her favourite child was dead?

The party moved into the church.

Edmund would be housed better in death than he had been in life, wasn't that old Hemmings's black joke when they had walked over to the church together? Burial would be under the flagstones of St Saviour – twenty pieces of silver had secured the place together with the tolling of the great church bell. Nobody was going to say that the Shakespeares did not look after their own. If the verger could have found where the bastard babe lay buried in the churchyard in the summer, a son might have rested with a father.

The body in its shroud was lowered into the space uncovered to receive it. Nobody would dig over Edmund's bones, Shakespeare had promised his brother.

We therefore commit the body to the ground, earth to earth...

London clay, not the red loam of Warwickshire.

... ashes to ashes, dust to dust...

A body which had once sported and pleased, an intelligence which had bantered and entertained, all lost, all gone and where to?

... in sure and certain hope of the resurrection to eternal life...

If only a man could be sure.

... blessed are the dead which die in the Lord...

Had Edmund died in the Lord?

Shakespeare had not been there when he did. He was in the playhouse, rehearsing a play for the Court at Christmas when the news came. They said that all men begged for salvation at the end and called for their mother. Did Edmund? Call for their mother?

In the alehouse near to the playhouse the mood was sombre among the small group of actors gathered to drink to the memory of the departed.

'Will you send word to your mother?' Hemmings asked the bereaved man. 'Has she lost others before?'

The likelihood was that she must have.

'I was the first to survive,' Shakespeare said. 'Two died before. There was a girl later who died, a sister, Anne...'

Another ghost knocked at the door of his memory. Hers. And then another – his only boy, his son and heir Hamnet. Did he rest in the Lord?

Hemmings said the not-to-be-spoken.

'The saddest part is, Ned never made the most of his gifts.'

It was true, Shakespeare acknowledged, the boy had talent, looks, he had belonged on the stage in a way that plenty of men didn't, men like himself. Had his rare gift scorched him?

'I shall tell her myself,' he said in answer to the earlier question.

'Ah!' Hemmings said, meaning how inconvenient that might be, to lose Shakespeare to Stratford again when he had only just returned.

'I'll take the two plays with me, finish the one off, resolve the other.'

'Any thoughts?' Hemmings asked.

'About the *Timon* play? There's nothing to say.'

'You'll see Wilkins about *Pericles* before you go?'

Argue with a novice writer, one with 'ideas' who wouldn't take advice kindly?

'If I must,' Shakespeare said.

'Oi, watch where you're going!'

Palmer's target was a pair of boys who had almost knocked him down onto the thick ice of the river, sliding past, rags bundled around their feet. The cold air which rushed into his lungs had a fierce, biting quality. It was colder than he could ever remember.

Who could blame them, he thought, watching the backs of the ragamuffins? Few others were enjoying the cold frost – not the watermen for sure who relied on the river for their trade or anyone else on land trying to make their way along frigid, rutted pathways at risk to life and limb.

All the same, traders were making the best of it, a 'frost fair' they called it, setting out stalls on the ice, keeping warm by coal-filled braziers, bright flames of fire flickering over and reflecting off the dark-glazed water.

One of them he recognised, and she him.

'Try my pies sweet'eart?' she called out to him with a wink.

Palmer went over to her.

'Deserting your favourite pitch?'

Alice usually sold from near St Paul's Cathedral.

'This is where the business is, darlin', fingers too cold for books an' all that over there.'

Seeing her reminded him of Ellen.

'Might you be looking for a helper?' he asked.

She gave him a 'not likely' look.

'Sorry, dearie, we keep it in the family.'

As far as he knew, 'the family' meant her alone. Palmer consoled himself with a pie, baked mutton – salty, greasy, warming. He told her a version of Ellen's story.

'She your piece?' the vendor speculated.

Palmer shook his head. He told her about the child on the way.

'Oh, better and better!' she laughed.

'I'm beginning to think that her only way out is to find a husband.'

'What, her with a loaf already bakin'? What sort of man'd want that? The wrong sort, there bein' a distinct shortage of Josephs about nowadays. Why you bothered about her anywise?'

Palmer repeated the question to himself, why was he? Because he bore her a responsibility, for pulling her out of the river for one.

'She'll have to go on the parish,' the pie-woman said.

'No,' Palmer said, 'she won't do it, same as she wouldn't get rid of the problem in the first place.'

'I see,' the pie-woman said, 'the daft sort!'

Maybe, Palmer told himself, different in a way that made him look out for her.

'Why not take her on yerself?'

Palmer did not know whether to laugh or cry.

'... no, silly, not as a 'usband, as a *servin'* woman. That way you gets her service, you gets serviced too if you wants an' there ain't no marriage service necessary neither! I hear as you're an officer of the Court these days. You can't be short of a few pennies!'

She gave him a mock curtsey.

Palmer hoped it wouldn't come to that.

'You misunderstand what I'm saying.'

Shakespeare was not happy to find himself on his own with an angry writer in front of him.

'I have no desire to change the work you've done so far,' he told George Wilkins, 'bar a suggestion here and there which you can take or leave as you please.'

'So why won't you let me get on with the scheme of the play as I planned it?'

Wilkins was clenching his fists, Shakespeare couldn't help noticing.

'My colleagues are not happy with it.'

'And you? What do you think?'

So there was no escape. Shakespeare took a deep breath.

'My colleagues are experienced men of the theatre, they know what works and what doesn't. They've made their views clear ... and yes, I agree with them.'

'I cannot write what they want.'

... meaning a climax with a princess rescued from a brothel, her virtue intact. If there was to be redemption, it was to be on Wilkins's terms, terms of dramatic truth to his mind. They had argued it backwards and forwards for half an hour now. Dramatic truth...

'George, you must understand, to put on your play is going to be costly. You're calling for a sackful of extra effects, item the revelation scene at the end. It's private theatre stuff, Inigo Jones stuff for the sort of paying audience we don't have at the Globe. Perhaps it's our fault,' he pretended to admit, 'but the public theatre is not ready for it, our audiences are not ready for it.'

A dangerous, glittering look came into the disappointed man's eyes.

'Shame on you,' he said.

'I'm sorry?'

'Shame on you!'

Shakespeare saw again the clenching and unclenching fists. He tried another approach.

'Look, apart from the rest, we'd never get it past the censor.'

'Aha!'

What did that mean, Shakespeare asked himself?

'There's a new man in the Revels office,' Wilkins said, 'a patron of my *establishment*.'

Shakespeare had heard, from Hemmings – Palmer, an old trouble and not, it was devoutly to be wished, to become a present one.

'We know him, it doesn't change our opinion, Tilney's still the man, and once he isn't, then it will be Buc.'

'We could grease the new man's palm.'

Shakespeare was about to laugh at the joke when he realised that the suggestion was serious.

'No,' he said.

There was no way he was going to grease Palmer's hand or any other part of him.

'So, you've lost your nerve,' Wilkins sneered, 'the hangman of Cordelia, the strangler of, what's-her-name – Desdemona ... the mutilator of poor Lavinia. You baulk at a virgin being popped in a bawdy house?'

It was pointless for Shakespeare to explain that the censor would never allow a royal princess to be sluiced on the public stage, not when the King had a daughter of his own. It was all too gross, a step too far.

'So is there no *goodness* in life?' Shakespeare heard himself say, asking himself as much.

The man opposite began to laugh.

'You're going soft, Mr Shakespeare. As for my *Pericles*, I'll take it that it's a no.'

Shakespeare gave a sharp nod of the head.

'I'll take it elsewhere,' Wilkins threatened.

'It's no longer yours, it's ours, money has passed.'

There *was* something he could do with it, Shakespeare began to think, more than just giving old chorus Gower a broader gait in his verse, slowing down the frenetic scene changes, avoiding the punctuation of one line proverbs. The story did have a certain magical imagination – he could see it if Wilkins couldn't, or couldn't make it happen.

It would be a challenge to the company – to bring off the scenic effects and show the people what the public theatre could do to match its private competitors, especially if the plan for the Blackfriars playhouse was to go ahead. Yes, perhaps this *Pericles* was the key to taking on the competition and beating them ... but it had to have hope, *goodness*, virtue triumphing even if, because, everybody knew that wasn't how life went. Nobody came to the playhouse to see the grim realities of everyday life rehearsed in front of them without some sort of hope.

'You haven't answered me,' Wilkins said.

'We'll keep it to hand,' Shakespeare shrugged. 'You never can tell in the theatre.'

~ 8 ~

'MR SHAKESPEARE'S no sooner back than he's gone again!'

Tilney's complaint echoed around the bare canvas walls of the Banqueting House in Whitehall.

Palmer was looking elsewhere. Workmen were setting up the stage on wheels at the centre of this tent of a building for another of Jonson and Jones's engine-driven masques. The built spectacle was as important as the text. He already knew from Tilney that it was most of the cost.

'You have your ear to the ground,' Tilney shouted over the clunks and clanks of the setting up. 'Is the man Shakespeare past it?'

Palmer had already had an unctuous encounter with Hemmings.

'... gone down to the country, family matters ... finishing off *two* plays, starting another ... *plenty* of material left in him.'

Palmer told Tilney what he had heard.

'He's taken the *Pericles* piece over,' he added.

'Probably no bad thing,' Tilney grunted. 'I didn't like the sound of the Wilkins man. So let's wait and see what we get from Mr Shakespeare.'

'He was in yowr care!'

The old woman in the corner of the kitchen in the modest family home in Stratford was adamant. Shakespeare felt like a schoolboy who had carelessly lost a sibling he was sent out to bring home from school.

'He was his own man,' he replied, 'he went his own way, he refused any further help from me until near the end.'

'He should never a' gone to London,' the old woman insisted, 'yow should never a' taken him.'

There was no answer to that. She was wrong, Shakespeare doggedly insisted in his head, but what could you tell a mother hearing of a son's death, a grown son too?

He had wanted to tell of the hard time he'd had coming home, the land hidden under a coverlet of grey ice, bare, leafless trees, their branches pointing starkly at the snow-burdened skies. A horse had slipped and gone lame under him on the treacherous, ungiving ground. Plague, politics and bad weather had so far marked King James's reign. None of that would mean a thing to the woman in front of him, not when compared to the death of her youngest boy, her Benjamin.

'I buried him well,' was all he could say, knowing that a good burial meant much in the minds of the old, 'a grave in the church, mourners, priest and the great bell tolling.'

Her face told him what she was thinking, that the new faith did not impress her. Where were the Latin words and the incense? Where were the masses for the dead so that Edmund did not disappear in death, forgotten?

She watched her son, her eldest, watching her.

'Must a' cost yow,' she offered him in consolation.

The news that his daughter Susanna was taken to bed, the baby coming, reached him in his chamber on a cold, dank February day.

'Has the midwife been sent for?' he asked the servant, knowing that it was all in hand – her husband the Doctor was at home, deliberately not out riding on his rounds.

Now it was women's work. Even the good Doctor was excluded.

Shakespeare prayed to whatever held human fortune in its palm that his daughter would come through safely and the child be born healthy.

He needed to occupy his mind. His eyes turned to the papers in front of him, one a neat pile, *Coriolanus*, finished, a warrior gone down to the house of his fathers in payment for his pride. It would play well. Burbage would shine in the heroic, martial part and there were at least six other good roles for the senior members of the company. If the hero's young wife had defeated him, it was because the hero's stern mother took the stage from her.

'Must a' cost yow' – shame he couldn't put that into Volumnia's mouth!

Another pile was thinner, lower, scratched and blotched, screeds of prose breaking into verse as the inspiration took him, but not often enough. He couldn't get the hang of his man – Timon, the rich and foolish Athenian deserted by his hangers-on when his riches vanished. The scheme was good, Thomas Middleton's scheme, another writer he was trying to encourage, about the perils of the over-lavish hand, the greed of those on the take from him, his fall, his inevitable fall, his railing against fate and the ingratitude of men. What then? Where did the golden boy Alcibiades fit? Their golden boy was dead, Edmund was dead. Who would play Alcibiades now?

Was that a woman's cry, somewhere in the house? Susanna in her labour? He had been at home for the birth of his three, Susanna first and then the twins. He remembered those sounds of women's pain. He could do no more about it now than he could then.

A third pile of papers drew his attention. It was *Pericles* needing to be made magical. Was he still alchemist enough? He pulled the papers towards him. He found the hero washed up on the shores of a foreign city, then nothing but blank parchment where Wilkins had stopped.

Words formed and reformed in his mind, overleaping prose straight into verse. He intoned them out loud before he wrote them down.

Yet cease your ire, you angry stars of heaven!

A woman's cry interrupted him again.

He shook it out of his head before it could drive out the words it had been forming.

Wind, rain and thunder, remember earthly man
Is but a substance that must yield to you...

More verses came. *Timon* could wait. Could Susanna?

He made his way down to the kitchen in the grand house. He found the Doctor, Susanna's husband, warming himself by the fire.

The look on the younger man's face was one of worry.

'It's a hard labour,' he told his father-in-law. 'The child will not come.'

'Where is my wife?' Shakespeare asked, expecting to have found her in the kitchen.

'With the women, helping.'

It was a surprise after all her years of ill-health and wandering wits, ever since the loss of their boy a dozen years before.

'It's her daughter. Shock, urgency may have this effect. We should be grateful,' the Doctor said.

No, Shakespeare thought, we shall only be grateful if Susanna is saved.

His mind went back to Pericles beached up on the shore, and to Thaisa his wife, at risk of dying in childbirth. He would go back to work on her revival, restore her to her husband! This would be his invocation, his means of aid to his own daughter in her distress.

'Tell me once there is news,' he said to Dr Hall before leaving him to write her salvation.

A brisk knocking at the door interrupted him in the late hours. He opened it to see his wife standing in front of him.

'It's a girl!'

'And Susanna?'

'Tired ... very tired, but well, well as can be expected.'

So not a boy then, not the heir male to inherit, if not the name, the wealth he was carefully, laboriously piling up.

'The Doctor is with her?'

'He's with her,' Anne Shakespeare repeated.

Shakespeare found him in his daughter's lying-in room. His presence justified the uncustomary intrusion of a second male into this province of women.

'A healthy girl,' the Doctor said.

The new grandfather looked over to where his daughter lay, half sleeping, next to her a tiny, ruddy face peaking out of a mass of cloth, making no noise.

'And Susanna?' he asked.

'It was a hard labour,' the Doctor said, at the same time implying something else.

'Tell me,' Shakespeare said.

'I doubt,' the Doctor began, 'from what the midwife told me, I doubt if there will be more.'

No son, no grandson … both men looked at each other, thinking the same.

'What shall she be called?' the Doctor asked, deferring to his father-in-law.

The older man paused to think.

'Elizabeth.'

His mother was a Mary but the world had passed from the Marys to the Elizabeths. Now it belonged to James, whose daughter was Elizabeth. Elizabeth lived on in her, and in the newborn in front of them.

'Elizabeth Hall,' the Doctor confirmed.

A terrible childbed…

He scratched the opening words down as he imagined a royal mother, her husband-prince standing over her in grief, her body about to be consigned to the waves from a storm-tossed ship. We'll save her later on, he said to himself, we'll save her.

His imagination turned to the mother's baby.

Mild... mild be your life, quiet and gentle your conditions.

What would Elizabeth Hall live to see? What would she become? With money behind her, she should become more than her mother, much more than her grandmother. Elizabeth Hall should grow to be a woman of rank and consequence.

A contradicting note in his head distracted him. It took him back to his writing.

SPLISH-SPLOSH, splish-splosh...

The childish phrase dogged Palmer's thoughts as he struggled through the streets on his way home. The great melt had brought floods of iced water mixed with mud and with effluent from beasts and men. The evil mixture swamped his boots, sparing him only the stink in the cold conditions. The liquid slid greasily around his toes.

He had avoided the river, coming back from Whitehall. The river was high, the currents approaching London Bridge more treacherous than ever. Was he getting old, did age bring about a greater desire to live on at all costs? He was tired, that much was sure.

The long Christmas season was over, and with it the nightly Court entertainments. The play by William Shakespeare had been *Coriolanus*, performed in the absence of the writer 'attending his daughter who has just given birth to his first grandchild', Hemmings explained when asked.

Tilney had shared his thoughts about its content with Palmer in advance, trying to teach his new officer something about the trade of licensing.

'The democrats in the play are no better than they should be, the people fickle as one might expect, the patrician a most reasonable advocate, wouldn't you say? A conciliator, quite in the mould,' Tilney said, leaving Palmer in no doubt whose mould he meant – King James's.

'What about Coriolanus's treason?' Palmer asked him.

Tilney waved the question away.

'He is persuaded to do the right thing in the end, in sparing Rome and he pays the price with his life. What could be more satisfactory?'

Palmer was now splashing his way into Turnmill Street, the sluggish sound of the old sewerine Fleet on his left adding to his general sense of inundation. On his right, he heard voices raised, from Wilkins's place. Was that surprising? Palmer trudged onwards.

A woman's voice soared above the internal hubbub, rising to a shriek. Palmer closed his ears. The voice screamed again, a terrible scream. It stopped Palmer in his tracks. Was it Ellen? He had promised her safety. He had done nothing much about securing it.

He made his way back to the door. The voice screamed again. He pushed the door open.

In front of him, Ellen lay sprawled on the floor, clutching the heavy load in her belly. Over her stood Wilkins, vicious eyes turned towards the unwelcome intrusion. Ellen stretched out a pleading hand in Palmer's direction.

'What do you want?' Wilkins snarled.

''E kicked me baby!' Ellen managed to gasp out.

There was no shame in Wilkins's eyes, Palmer saw, only deadness. 'What are you going to do about it?' the eyes said.

Ellen crawled, groaning as she moved towards Palmer. The sight appeared to amuse her employer. Palmer saw him flex his right leg. His kick went home, Ellen groaned again. Bile began to dribble from the corners of her mouth.

Palmer executed three quick paces bringing his knee full force into the small of the back of the woman-beater. Wilkins gave a cry of wounded astonishment as he dropped to his knees. Palmer pulled his head back by the hair.

'One move and I'll beat your brains out,' he threatened.

Keeping an eye on the groaning man, Palmer turned to Ellen.

'You have to get up,' he urged her.

There was no time to be sympathetic.

Ellen's eyes told him that she didn't think she could.

Palmer stooped and held out a helping forearm.

Ellen reached up, took it and hauled herself to her knees. A second huge effort brought her to her feet, leaning heavily on Palmer. She was still light enough for him to manage her, he calculated.

'Put your arm around my neck,' he urged her, making sure that he had at least one hand free, for the knife he carried in his boot.

Wilkins had pulled himself up into a semi-slumped position, his back against a wall.

'Take her,' he grimaced with pain, 'and I'll fix you.'

'Fix an officer of the Crown?' Palmer said.

He heard Ellen gasp into his ear.

'Christ Jesu, I'm bleedin'.'

There was nowhere else for Palmer to half-haul, half-carry her back except to his tenement chamber nearby, no bed in which to lay the girl except the old Palmer heirloom. He laid her on her back, offered her a rag dipped in water, looked away while she lifted her skirts, heard the stifled sobbing. He thought he knew what it meant, not good.

'Shall I go get the local woman?' he asked.

His mind went back to where they had first met, by an Oxford river, with the birth of a healthy daughter, a child she had deserted for an actor, a Shakespeare, only to come to rest with a Wilkins and his fists and his boots.

'No,' she wailed. 'Don't leave me.'

Palmer saw the blood between her legs pulsing out over her skirt and livid bruises beginning to form on her thighs. He went to find a shirt, his other one to give to her to staunch the flow and to protect his bed.

An internal spasm marked itself on her face as she sank back.

Palmer took the shirt from her hand. The blood was still flowing fast. Was the child coming? What could he do about the bleeding? He had seen it in war, men wounded in the lungs or in the gut, there was nothing could be done if it didn't stop of its own accord. Would it help if the baby came? He pressed his hands on her belly, she winced, turning her head aside.

'Don't leave me,' she repeated, the voice huskier, failing.

The blood wouldn't stop, the shirt was sodden and so was the palliasse beneath her, dripping onto the oaken floor making a ruby-brown pool. Palmer ripped the shirt off his back. It did no good. He felt a shock course through Ellen's body. Palmer knew what it meant, he had seen it in war. He heard the rattle in her throat. The blood would soon stop now, he knew, soon stop…

What to do with the body?

He cleaned the blood from the corpse as best he could. The body on his bed was no longer Ellen as far as he was concerned but, in disposing of her, there were others to consider. The Davenants? Maybe. More to the point, little

Miracle. Shouldn't she know, one day, where her mother was buried and that it had been done in the right way? He was her godfather after all. One day there might be questions, one day he might have to answer them.

For reasons he could not explain, he lit his last remaining candles and placed them at her head and feet.

Something between conscience and fear of consequences took him where he needed to go, to the sexton in the church nearby, someone open to a palm being greased, someone with a secret which gave the investigator a hold over him. There was to be no inquest and no formal record. What would it achieve? There had been no witnesses, or none who would speak. He had taken Ellen away, she had died in his room. The irony was not lost on him, that if he had left her where she was, Wilkins would be the one facing the problem he was now.

Palmer's help to Ellen had robbed her of justice.

'Have to be burial at night, under the old yew tree,' the man told him. 'Yes, I can find a priest to do the necessary – for a fee – and ask no questions. No, the name won't be set down in the register. You reckoning on being here?'

Ordinarily Palmer would have said no, but he knew he had to, to make sure sexton and priest did what was promised and to note where the burial place was. He said he would.

'And I'll need you to send the bier round to my chamber, after dark.'

It was late in the day, after nightfall, when Palmer and the sexton trundled the transport towards St James's Churchyard. Such a sight was not unusual in these days of the plague coming and going. The sexton gave Palmer a look to ask whose the body was, wrapped up in a winding cloth but with no face showing.

'No-one you need know about,' Palmer said, a new shirt itching his back.

Except that he did. The sexton was one of Wilkins's customers, that was his secret. He would know about Ellen's leaving, but would he ask? If he asked, would Wilkins tell? Palmer doubted it, not if it meant the man risking Wilkins's wrath over his complicity.

He stood a little way off while the solemnities were executed and the body interred with no sign left other than a low mound of freshly dug earth. Palmer settled the accounts of the two men, smelling the spirits on the breath of the priest as he did and where the money would soon be spent. He sent no word to the Davenants in Oxford. One day, such a thing might be said because it should not be written down.

Revenge? He thought hard. Was there a way to put Wilkins in front of the Justices? The man was a bully, a whoremaster and a murderer. But the same thoughts returned – where did she die, what was the evidence, who were the witnesses? Palmer had no trust in the processes of the Law. It too often chased the last man seen.

Might he take it into his own hands? A precedent reminded itself, of how he had dealt with pink-faced Lanier – husband of Emilia, the infatuation of his youth – whose foolish face he'd reshaped and with good cause. And so? The man had turned successful in this new world, so what was the point?

All the same, he set off to confront Wilkins with the result of the beating he had given a girl now lying stone cold dead under the earth.

Wilkins wasn't there. What Palmer found was the wife.

'He's gone away, business he said,' she said, avoiding Palmer's eyes.

She was unclear when he would be back. Her eyes swivelled away from him. She had demons of her own and just a little respite from them until her husband returned.

Palmer said nothing about Ellen's death. He went home to clean up the mess, then he brooded in his chamber. What had he the power to do? A sudden fearful recollection came to mind – the sonnets, hidden under the bed! Half-panicked, he went down on his knees to release them from their hiding place. He ripped the parcel open. Only one drop of Ellen's blood had penetrated the package, half drying already, blotting an opening line.

From fairest creatures we desire increase...

The blot occluded the word 'fair.'

Palmer rocked back on his creaking haunches. Fair? Ellen?

Part of him despised the girl's stupidity. 'No better than she should be' did not excuse her. But this? Violent death, leaving nothing more behind her than a small blot on a line of verse?

Two lives blotted out?

There was something left, the child Miracle in Oxford. It was something for Palmer to hold onto.

'Mr Shakespeare is back in town.'

The news came from Edmund Tilney when an unusually sober Palmer reported for duty.

'... and he has the *Pericles* play.'

It was decided to hold the reading in the Blackfriars Theatre.

'There's a move afoot,' Tilney confided to Palmer, 'for the King's Men to go in there.'

'Isn't there a children's company there already?'

'Yes, the Children of the Queen's Revels, but there's been trouble.'

... accusations about children of good families being pressed into the company, difficulties with a too satirical play involving Ben Jonson which the authorities had taken umbrage over – where there was trouble Jonson's name was regularly to be found, that much Palmer knew from experience.

'Do we approve of boys' companies?' he asked.

To Palmer's mind, grammar school plays with boys performing classics in Latin or Greek to improve their command of the languages was one thing, mouthing the satire of Jonson in the sex-ridden, roughhouse language of the day, quite another.

'They are a fashion,' Tilney contented himself with answering.

The boy-players had powerful backers. A Court official was wise not to take a political position on these matters; it was more practicable to interpret his job as sensibly as the times permitted. All this Palmer would learn, Tilney was certain, if he *would* learn.

'We present *Pericles, Prince of Tyre*,' proclaimed the presenter from his place in the centre of the stage, 'in which the illustrious potentate, travelling to Antioch to seek the hand of its princess, must decipher a great riddle, the secret of which, discovered, would see him put to death. And so he flees over the sea to Tarsus and is brought by shipwreck to Pentapolis. Here in knightly joust he wins the hand of Pentapolis's princess

– Thaisa is her name – with whom he sails away to claim his rightful throne of Tyre, only to lose her – or so he thinks – in childbirth in a mighty storm...'

William Shakespeare spoke in flowing form. There was no sign of Wilkins, Palmer was pleased and also relieved to see. It was one thing to deal with him in anger, another to summon up courage from nothing.

Tilney interrupted.

'What's new in this?' he asked, thinking of the need to feed the Court's appetite for novelty.

'Romance,' Shakespeare replied, 'spectacle – a great riddle scene, a pageant of knights, music of the spheres, the goddess Diana in her temple.'

'Why, it sounds to me as if you've gone into the masque business!'

Tilney turned to Palmer for applause, only Palmer was too slow to realise it. The joke fell flat.

'Well put, Master,' Shakespeare intervened to flatter the old man, 'but the play's still the thing, brightened for the modern taste by magical effects which we shall bring off well.'

'And the royal princess, the one you have put into a brothel, she survives *intact*?'

'More, Master, she becomes virtue's beacon, converting all around her, even,' Shakespeare said, 'the governor of the place who comes to use her.'

Tilney coughed.

'Yes, well, boys will be boys...'

The room relaxed around his little joke.

'... and we understand that virtue is doubly rewarded?'

'... by our hero's reunion with his wife, thought dead in childbirth.'

Ellen's ghost came up in front of Palmer's eyes and with it a nausea at the base of his throat.

'Wilkins,' Palmer spoke up, without Tilney's approval, 'Wilkins is not here.'

'He is not needed here.' Hemmings intervened to say. 'It's true he came up with the story and a few, a very few scenes but Mr Shakespeare has taken it over – our *best* and most *experienced* talent – so that this fine subject can receive full justice. No, Wilkins is not needed.'

Not now or ever. Justice for Ellen no-name fanned at the fire burning in Palmer's brain.

~ 10 ~

P LAGUE.
As if it wasn't enough to have suffered the coldest winter ever remembered, the spring thaw brought back the perennial disease. It came with a fearsome vigour.

When the weekly number of deaths in the capital quickly surpassed the legislated number, the pestilence was officially proclaimed.

Palmer didn't need Tilney to tell him the consequence – the closure of the playhouses and other places of public entertainment.

'The players are a resilient lot,' Tilney added, as if to convince himself that they would not be put out of business by this latest attack of the disease.

Palmer was called in by Buc.

'There may be a surge in plays put out for printing,' Buc explained, 'if the acting companies need to raise income during the closedown. I suggest you check with the Stationers' company what they are expecting then talk to the printing houses. They need to know that the texts must come to us first, before publication. Plague is no excuse for evading regulations.'

Was Buc looking to drum up business while Tilney suffered, Palmer asked himself? Printed plays meant licensing fees for him and increased influence for the new man at a time when the work of the acting companies, Tilney's work was under threat. Was the younger wolf circling?

As spring gave way to summer, the disease continued in force with the numbers of deaths stubbornly above the prescribed number. Palmer consulted his snout in the Stationers' Hall. The information he got back was interesting –

a *King Lear* registered the previous year was due to be published. The publishers were not men with any 'form', his informant let him know, although the text was rumoured to be a memorised one, that is, 'it does not come from the script held by the King's Men'.

So the *Lear* publishers were men on the make, Palmer concluded. All the same, Buc would want to see their text.

Of more interest to him was the second tip.

'You should try Ned Blount,' the snout told him. 'He's the publisher of choice for your poets of quality. Word is going round that Blount's interested in Shakespeare for a new venture.'

'Where do I find this Blount?' Palmer asked.

'Usual place, St Paul's Churchyard.'

Blount could wait, Palmer decided. He wanted a break. The plague combined with the reduced activity in the office of the Revels granted him as good an opportunity as he would get for some time. He also had a duty to perform, in memory of Ellen.

He could not forget her. The atmosphere in his chamber still carried her impression. The oaken floor beneath his bed continued to bear a stain from her blood. The new palliasse was not as comfortable as the old one it had replaced, smuggled out at dead of night and dumped into the Fleet nearby in order to avoid awkward questions. He had watched it sink slowly into the treacly black waters, swallowing the evidence.

Wilkins was back in his tavern, Palmer had seen when passing by. He passed up the temptation to confront him. He would only do that, he decided, when he was in the mood to do him permanent damage.

In May he took leave of absence. He rode out of the capital in the direction of Oxford and the Davenant family who had cared for Ellen and for her little girl, Miracle. She would be approaching her fourth birthday at the end of summer, he reminded himself, if she still lived; he had no reason to think she didn't – there had been no untoward word in response to his, finally sent to the Davenants, on Ellen's death.

The countryside, forgotten country was refreshing in its greenness, carpeted with flowers, butter yellow, laundry white and celestial blue. The sun stood high in the sky, the breeze fresh turning to sharp if a passing cloud obscured the sun's warmth. It was the landscape of his youth, a world apart from London.

What would a girl of three turning four be like, Palmer wondered? How much changed from the baby into the child and on the way to little womanhood? He'd had no sisters, none that lived; he was the only Palmer to reach adulthood from his parents' brood – not that they had been many with a mother dying young. Perhaps his father's harshness had been formed out of her loss. The man had turned to God to the exclusion of humanity.

The journey took him an extended day's hard riding with a single change of horse. In Oxford he found the Tavern easily enough, in the Cornmarket. Inside was the same laconical landlord, John Davenant with the same dry welcome.

Jane Davenant was more welcoming. Palmer was pleased to see her, handsome as ever.

'How long is it since we saw you last?' she said, echoing his own thoughts.

'Two years?' he hazarded.

Her grey eyes suddenly welled with tears, for Ellen.

'Is the little girl...' Palmer put in quickly to cut off the flow.

'Oh yes!' Jane Davenant smiled, 'very much alive, and flourishing,' laughter drying her eyes.

It was best to talk about Miracle.

'Her mother's looks,' the landlady told him, 'but she's an old head on young shoulders, a little busybody, keen on her letters, such of them as she's learned from me.'

'Doesn't she miss her mother?' Palmer asked.

'I've always treated her as my own, and it was a year ago Ellen left...'

'With an actor,' Palmer said, 'brother of Shakespeare,' wondering if she knew.

'We weren't sure. It was only a matter of time before she took up and took off with somebody. It explains one thing.'

Palmer asked her what that was.

'... we haven't seen Mr Shakespeare since Ellen's disappearance. He always used to stay with us on his way to and from Stratford. Tell me, what really happened to Ellen?'

The look on Palmer's face told her as much as she wanted to know.

He took a small bag from inside his doublet.

'As Miracle's godfather,' he explained, handing the money over, an act of expiation to Ellen's ghost.

Since it was already late in the day, he agreed to wait until the morning before he saw his god-daughter. She was brought into his chamber after he had taken his breakfast. The occasion made her shy by its unusualness and the sense that she was on display in front of a stranger.

Palmer lacked the skill to put her at her ease. She had Ellen's looks, he could see, especially the pale red hair. Would being brought up a Davenant to all intents and purposes change her fortunes, or was it true what the proverb said, that 'blood will out'?

Miracle stood where she was, coyly looking up at the grizzled man seated on a stool.

'What should she call you?' Jane Davenant, standing behind her asked him.

Palmer was at a loss.

Miracle broke the silence.

'Uncle Two-Names,' she shouted.

Jane Davenant laughed.

'Ellen used to say that's who you were.'

It was how Palmer had first come to them using an alias, William Henry the bookseller, in pursuit of Ben Jonson in Gunpowder time.

'Uncle Two-Names? It'll do,' he said.

Palmer didn't stay long in Oxford, enough to show willing and to accept hospitality, not so much that he was under the Davenants' feet or too much in their debt. He said nothing about his new work in the capital. The Davenants did not enquire.

When he saddled up to go, John Davenant spoke.

'There's plague in London, so they say.'

Can't bring you down twice, Palmer hoped, in memory of his own encounter with the pest and from what he had heard said here and there, old wives' tales like as not. Jane Davenant was holding the child up to wave goodbye, but not for too long – Miracle was getting too heavy. Her own boy William clung to her skirts, pleased at the thought of getting his mother – and Miracle – back once this stranger was gone.

With Oxford behind him, Palmer took the pace more easily back to London than on the way out, as if he was reluctant to return. He stopped in High Wycombe, taking time to pick out the sort of establishment he was looking for.

The maidservant who took him to his chamber gave him a frank, encouraging look – if he wanted anything, *anything at all*, he had only to call for her.

He pulled her towards him. She hoped that he was *gen'rous*.

Hers was the first woman's body he had touched since Ellen's dead carcass.

'Don't stop now,' the maidservant coaxed, pulling her skirts up, mounting his lap as she pushed him down onto a stool, her hand fishing towards his groin. He felt the surge, knew that what should happen would.

She reached down and drew him in. She smelled of honest work, the sweat of the day, a sweetish smell, like freshly baked cake. He saw that she had a blemish on one of her newly exposed breasts, like a stain from a pool of wine…

… or blood.

The memory of Ellen, bruised and bleeding imposed itself. All the lust drained out of him.

LONDON WAS STILL in the shadow of the plague when Palmer returned to it, fewer people in the streets.

The following morning he made an early start, heading for St Paul's Churchyard to pursue the publishers of plays as Buc had urged him to. He found the shop of Edward Blount, round by the north porch.

Blount was a man in his early forties, Palmer judged, approachable on the face of him.

'I'd heard there was a new man in the office,' the printer said, referring to Palmer's post in Tilney's team.

'Then you know that published plays must now be licensed too,' Palmer said.

The twinkle in the publisher's eyes told Palmer what he thought of yet another tax on his time and on his pocket – and that he would cope with it.

'I've not been much in the play-publishing business. Poetry, yes, and lexicology – dictionaries to ordinary folk – some history and travel...'

'Who would your poets be?' Palmer asked.

'In my apprenticeship, Spenser and Sidney, on my own, Kit Marlowe. Some call me the executor of his writing. I make it live. You know his work?'

'Dead, I heard. Anything of Shakespeare's?'

Blount looked at his interrogator with more interest.

'His poem *Phoenix and the Turtle* – mean anything to you? It's six or seven years old; not a lot of call for it, I must admit, but then, some sell, some don't.'

'So, no plans to publish any of his plays? I'd heard word that you might be.'

Blount smiled again.

'Publishing is a giddy world for gossip but, on this occasion, the rumours might be true. I'm interested in his *Anthony & Cleopatra*. Do you ... well, let's not bother with that,' he said kindly, sparing Palmer any further tests of his knowledge. 'It was well-received last year and it's had a good run on the stage. If I can persuade the King's Men to part with their script, which they may want to in the current conditions,' he said, 'then I shall publish it.'

'So you're not one for a pirated version,' Palmer said in a friendly way.

Blount shook his head.

'I like to think my authors can trust me, whether they be dead or alive. As for the Egyptian play, I intend to register my intention to publish with the guild. After that, what must I do?'

'Provide a proof script for licensing,' Palmer said. 'Sir George Buc's the man in charge when it comes to publishing. You can do it through me.'

'So it will go to Buc, not the Bishop's man.'

Blount appeared content enough with that.

Job done, Palmer thought. An idle question popped out.

'So what do you think the acting companies are going to do about the new plays they have on the stocks, given these present conditions?'

'Are there any?' Blount asked casually, giving the impression that it didn't matter to him one way or the other.

'There's a *Pericles*.'

Was it a leading question, or just a coincidence, Blount asked himself? He'd had a visit in the previous week from old John Hemmings of the King's Men with an unusual request...

'... if we help you with our Egyptian play, would you be interested in a couple of new ones we have, in case we choose not to produce them, in these difficult times?'

It had made the publisher suspicious when the veteran actor told him that they were by Shakespeare. He found it hard to believe. What he was being offered was either something very dodgy indeed or the publishing stroke of the young century. He had asked what they were and Hemmings had told him, beginning with one called *Timon of Athens*.

'More a piece to be read, we think, rather than played,' covering for the fact that Shakespeare had seemed to lose interest in it and left it unfinished; but not so unfinished that it mightn't have a value in the print market.

'The other one is *Pericles, Prince of Tyre*. This one's not a done deal, you understand, but we'd let you have first option so you could register your intention to publish.'

What was it that had sounded so fishy, the publisher asked himself? So fishy that he was reluctant to tell this inquisitive new officer of the Revels that he was preparing to register *Pericles* for publication as well as the Egyptian play.

'I heard that George Wilkins was writing *Pericles*,' Blount had challenged Hemmings.

Truth was, Wilkins had been to see him about it himself, in equally cloak-and-dagger style. Blount had given him the 'I'll give it serious thought' answer – Wilkins was not a man to upset, or so he'd heard, but he didn't like him and Blount liked to deal with men he liked.

Hemmings had come clean.

'Look, Shakespeare's taken *Pericles* over and we think it's a winner. Trouble is, there's nowhere to put it on, and if things go on as they are,' he said, referring to the plague, 'it could be the midwinter season at Court before we get our chance. Meantime, we *know* Wilkins isn't happy, and we hear he may want to spike our guns by publishing his own version. And let me tell you, Mr Blount, it'll never get past the censors, not the way Wilkins wants to write it.'

Blount looked back at Palmer who was waiting for an answer. He decided not to let him in on the deal he'd agreed with Hemmings, registration to keep it out of the hands of others, or the approach by Wilkins. The situation was complicated enough as it was.

'It's my guess that the players'll hold over *Coriolanus* and *Pericles* for the Court season at Christmas,' he said, honestly enough.

'Who else is looking to be in the play publishing business?' Palmer asked him, interested in what was to come rather than what was already known.

The question reminded him of a tip-off from his snout in the Stationers hall, that there had been a recent registration by another publisher, for a work by Ben Jonson, a masque. This publisher had also handled other Jonson pieces.

When Blount waved the question away, Palmer speculated the name.

'What about Thomas Thorpe? Know where I might find him?'

The answer was not far away in the churchyard at the shop of one William Aspley.

Whereas Blount was frank, to Palmer's mind there was something slippery about Thorpe when he caught up with him – or just plain odd? He could have sworn that Thorpe would have slid out of the back door if he'd known who he was and what he wanted.

Palmer checked the man's record.

'Bit of this, bit of that,' Thorpe said, and when pinned down, 'this one and that one.'

Behind the large, solicitous eyes which never seemed quite to focus, Palmer wondered if the man wasn't laughing at him.

'Let's try a name – Ben Jonson,' he said.

'True, true,' Thorpe admitted. 'Mr Jonson trusts me to present his works how he would himself if he was a printer. He's a stickler for his own proof-reading, mind! Two plays and a pair of masques,' he said, his eyes darting around, anywhere but in direct contact with Palmer's.

'Anything by Shakespeare?

'Shakespeare? Yes, yes, *Much Ado* and ... and ... *Henry Fourth* ... the part with the Boar's Head tavern and merry Sir John Falstaff.'

'What are your plans for the future?' Palmer asked, explaining the need to submit intended publications for approval.

'Mr Jonson's masques. I expect they'll keep me busy.'

'No more Shakespeare?' Palmer asked.

'Yes, yes ... if offered. Have ... have you got any?'

Did he have some, Palmer repeated to himself in the street outside after the interview with Thorpe? Yes he did, those private sonnets. A canker of worms, he decided, trying to put them out of his mind.

What was more in his mind was his favourite Bell Inn in Carter Lane where he could rest his feet, wet his whistle and review his morning's work. In addition to the plans he'd heard from Blount, local intelligence had also revealed the likely printing of three other plays by Shakespeare. That made five, five fees to the censors, good news to take back to Buc.

What he hadn't expected was to find the Chief Minister's official sitting in his own regular spot in the back room.

'Looking for you,' the landlord confirmed, 'second time 'e's been 'ere.'

Palmer was surprised. The man knew where to find him, care of the Revels office. Or perhaps he wanted to talk away from official ears?

'Ah, Mr Palmer!'

The Whitehall man carried something close to pleasure in his voice.

'Sorry if I've been difficult to find,' Palmer apologised, 'I've been on leave.'

Court officers, he had learned, did not take holidays, they took leave – it sounded grander.

The official lowered his voice.

'Have you heard the great news?'

What news could he mean? There was plague in the capital, the King still lived, Palmer was in work, everything was right with the world, everything except the continuing existence of George Wilkins. He didn't want any other news, great or otherwise.

'My Lord Salisbury,' the official whispered, referring to the Chief Minister, 'is to be made Lord Treasurer, just as his great father once was.'

It was the ultimate moneybags job, and Palmer said so.

'There's the paradox,' the official said, 'the coffers are as near empty as makes no difference.'

Palmer leaned back on his stool, surprised, and yet not so. Old Elizabeth had run a tight ship, King James thought he did too, except that he kept handing out land and titles and money to whoever pleased him, especially his latest boyfriend. It was widely complained about, especially when the largesse went Scotswards, for example to Robbie Carr.

'And how is his lordship?' Palmer asked.

The official was apologetic.

'Hideously busy – he remains Chief Minister, if I didn't say.

The official droned on in a low voice, about raising customs duties for the first time in fifty years and introducing new ones, instituting a review of crown lands and beginning to improve the rental return. After five minutes, Palmer had lost him and was looking longingly at his empty pint pot. In desperation, he interrupted the official's flow.

'What is all this to do with the Revels?'

'I was coming to that,' the official said.

Palmer waited patiently.

'Now,' the official said, 'the Lord Treasurer...'

He spoke the title in such a marvelling way. The lustre from high office was shedding its light all around, including on the old official.

'... is writing a series of treatises for the King...'

'Treatises?' Palmer queried.

'More than memoranda,' the official explained, sharing a sly glance with his listener, 'more like essays...'

Palmer recognised the fashionable French term.

'... essays designed to inculcate the principles of, ah, sound finance into the King's thinking.'

How on earth did that affect the Revels?

'A little bird tells us...'

Which one, Palmer wondered?

'... that Mr Shakespeare is working on a play, about the pitfalls of over-generosity?'

Palmer pretended to know what the old official was talking about.

'The Timon story, out of Plutarch, *Timon of Athens*,' the official prompted him.

Palmer's mind went into furious over-activity. He hadn't heard much about this one, why hadn't he been told?

'I see,' he worked out as he spoke. 'So there is a value in parables?'

... for the King to be served a message in a softer, more digestible form.

'... I'll see what can be done.'

Timon of Athens, Palmer repeated in his head once he had sent the old official on his way. There would be opportunities enough to find out more when he met the actors in the course of his work; or maybe from Blount, the publisher. From Thorpe he doubted if he would get a straight answer on anything.

He was about to leave the Bell when another figure approached him from across the room. It took a beat or two between knowing that he knew the man to putting a name to him. It gave him no pleasure. He stood up, prepared for anything.

'Mr Lanier,' he said.

Alphonse Lanier owed him a beating for the one he'd taken in an alleyway in return for an attempt on Palmer's life, back in the days of the old Queen. Palmer was pleased to see that the nose on the big, pink face was still crooked from the encounter.

Lanier summoned service, ordering a couple of pots of beer.

'My wife Emilia has a proposition,' he began, once he had slaked his thirst with a long pull from the pot set down in front of him.

How much did Lanier ever know, Palmer wondered? That Emilia had been the bedmate of the old Lord Chamberlain, patron of the acting company since translated to glory as the King's Men – yes, because he'd been paid to take her off the noble lord's hands and to take on her expected child. But had she told him all the rest of it, about Shakespeare and Southampton and all those sonnets? If she had, was it a version bearing any relation to the truth?

'You have some papers of hers,' Lanier said.

He did, Palmer mentally agreed, sonnets, envois, wasn't that the fashionable term, from poet to his dark mistress. Did Lanier know what Emilia meant by 'papers'?

'She would like them back. We are prepared to pay.'

Why on earth would she do that, Palmer asked himself? He had paid her good money for them himself, seven years ago now, when the Chief Minister had first put him on their writer's tail.

'How much?' Palmer asked out of interest.

Lanier named a price roughly the same as what Palmer remembered paying her before. It was a nice try, he thought, but not enough. Any interested publisher would pay more and she would know that. For her to have decided to approach him, there must be a pressing reason, a reason why she could not risk them being in open circulation, with their story of lust and betrayal. The last time he had seen her was when he was on the Gunpowder case, she in the company of a noble lady to whom she was a companion. Lady Cumberland was religious and immaculate of reputation. Was that it? Was Emilia in need of turning spotless, of a kind of virgin rebirth?

'How is your wife?' Palmer asked Lanier.

'She's well,' he said, 'living in the country with Lady Cumberland and her daughter. The boy's with her,' Lanier added.

Not 'our' boy, Palmer noted.

'He must be coming on a young man,' Palmer said. 'What are your plans for him?'

'Court musician. He already has many of the skills. My brothers and I have taught him.'

Court musician? Just as this Alphonse Lanier had been before he got the ambition to turn gallant captain. He had served with Essex and Southampton against the Spaniards and in their ill-conceived rebellion against Crown and State. The reward for treason had been a money-making perk when the world turned upside down upon King James of Scotland coming into England. Such things never happened to the Palmers of this world...

... so, it was to be music for young Lanier then. Emilia played music too, Palmer recalled, his mind going back to youthful days in Kent and a young woman at her keyboard making noise with her fingers to drown out what he'd had a mind to ask her, a forest of sounds blanketing his sentimental words. Foolish days, Palmer reflected.

'Look Palmer,' Lanier began to bully, 'name a price and let's see how we go on.'

Let the man sweat, Palmer decided instead.

Lanier fidgeted, appearing to toss around in his mind whether he should tell Palmer what he had been forbidden to reveal.

'Emilia has ambitions.'

She'd always had those, Palmer thought, shape-shifting from bastard daughter of a musician to ward of a noble lady, then hop, hop, hop into the bed of one of the most powerful men in the kingdom. It hadn't been enough. She'd cast her eyes in the direction of a dangerous young darling, Southampton, until an inconvenient pregnancy brought the whole house of cards tumbling down and left her with nothing but to be married off to the fool in front of him.

'… her patroness encourages her in these ambitions. They are taking the form of …'

The form of what?

'… the form of religious verses – don't ask me to explain, Palmer, you know how it is, once they're too old for enjoying themselves on their backs they take to bothering God on their knees.'

The two men's eyes met unkindly. Lanier hurried on.

'There's a circle of ladies of rank,' he said, feeling his way forward in his explanation of something he himself was not sure that he comprehended. 'They share the same devotion as Lady Cumberland…'

Palmer bet that they did.

'… so Emilia's verse could be dedicated to them. Dedication leads to publication, don't ask me how – I've never read a book in my life if I could avoid it.'

'She thinks there's money in it, doesn't she,' Palmer said.

Palmer remembered something the old official had once told him, that Lanier's perk still was not being paid out in full. So, they needed money. And given the religious subject-matter, Emilia needed to wipe away any compromising proofs of her past life.

'There's something else, Palmer,' Lanier said. 'The Countess's daughter is about to marry. It will bring to an end mother and daughter's right to the tenure of their country home at Cookham and...'

'... that will send Emilia back to London, and to you?'

'Yes, that's about the sum of it. But don't you see, Palmer, it's not the money – though we could do with it, God knows. A book would keep Emilia in with her fine ladies. There is no way she can keep company with them once she is out of the noble household.'

'These ... papers,' Palmer began to say about the sonnets in his possession, 'they may not be the only copies.'

Which was possible, Palmer told himself. He thought he might have them all, but you never could tell in the murky world of writers and publishers.

Lanier appeared surprised to hear it.

'... and I have a difficulty,' Palmer added. 'I am now an officer of the Revels, I can't be seen to be dealing in certain sorts of ... matters, under the table.'

Not for that price and not yet.

'So what am I to tell Emilia?' Lanier asked.

For all his rough treatment of her, Palmer could see that her husband was afraid of her.

'Tell her, I will let her know.'

~ 12 ~

THE REGULAR JOURNEY home past Wilkins's tavern was provoking to Palmer.

Should he deal with Wilkins one dark night down an alleyway? He had killed men, yes, but in war or in self defence. Something in him drew the line at murder.

Life was going on inside the tavern, he could see, light reflecting through a suggestive red lattice window. There would be another girl or two in there, upstairs, treading where Ellen had, doing what she had done.

Palmer turned in his tracks. The clue to sorting Wilkins out might lay with the actors since the plague was now sporadic – there was talk of normal activity being allowed to resume which would mean the playhouses reopening. The actors could block Wilkins and his ambitions and he, Palmer could help them do it. But they could not deliver the revenge he needed.

He set his thoughts aside. There was the *Timon* play to think about, how he could meet the Chief Minister's needs for a parable for His Majesty on the subject of how *not* to handle money. If he managed it right, it meant money on the side for him.

Palmer headed back south to the river, and a wherry across to the recreations of Bankside.

At first he could find none of the actors in their regular alehouse. He was on his way out, resigned to a wasted mission when he heard the unusual laugh he remembered from another time and place, that curious Shakespeare whoop. He went back inside.

The laughter on Shakespeare's face froze when he saw who it was. Palmer knew he could not be ignored, not now that he was an officer of the Revels.

'I believe the proscription on the plays may soon be lifted,' Palmer said.

'So I hear.'

'So we shall be seeing your newly-licensed plays.'

Shakespeare said nothing in reply.

'Are you living round here now?' Palmer asked, assuming that he was, otherwise why would he be there when others of his company patently were not?

Shakespeare was reluctant to admit it. He was keeping on the room Hemmings had found for his late brother. It was more than just convenience. Somehow it maintained the bond, the shared presence with his dead brother. This was not something he was going to explain to anyone, least of all to the man in front of him.

'Wilkins thought you were still in – where was it? – Cripplegate, in Silver Street,' Palmer said.

The look on Shakespeare's face showed what he thought of George Wilkins. The King's Men had heard nothing more from him since the man's last interview with their chief writer. There had been rumours, that he was trying to sell his version of the play come what may, despite the money he had already taken from the actors for it. This was why Hemmings had gone to see a friendly publisher, Blount to see if they could get their version registered first.

'I'm in lodgings nearby,' Shakespeare said at last. 'Helps to be near my place of work, especially if it's about to reopen, as you say.'

But if the company took on the Blackfriars Theatre, that would be the place to be, on the north side of the river, a good area, maybe one in which to buy after all these years of lodging in the capital; one had to think for the long term, Shakespeare reminded himself. Property matched the span of any man and most often outlived him. His grand house in Stratford already had a hundred years of life and living in it before he bought it. Bricks and mortar certainly, even wattle and daub outlasted the weaker stuff of flesh and blood.

'*Timon of Athens*,' Palmer started to say, to see what reaction he would get. 'Let's assume you know what I mean – stop me if you don't.'

He pulled up a stool.

'I have received, in my official capacity you understand,' he said with a smile, '*interest* from a highly placed source, on behalf ... shall we say, of a figure of standing ... that the play should see the light of day. It should be licensed and performed.'

The man opposite kept his counsel – the play stood where it had for months, unresolved, set aside. Shakespeare had assigned the first half of it to the younger writer Middleton, one of several he needed to feed the appetite of the King's Men's audiences for the dozen and more new plays required every year. It wasn't what he now wanted to be writing, *Coriolanus* was the last of that vein. In taking over *Pericles* he had found liberation despite its poor parentage, and the chance to dream again.

Palmer waited him out. Shakespeare gave in.

'*Timon* doesn't work, Mr Palmer. I've left it mouldering in its grave. It's not the first to suffer that fate,' but he prayed it would be the last. There was only so much time left, not to be wasted.

Palmer tried tempting him.

'There may be special recognition, if you resurrect it.'

The Chief Minister paid well, everyone knew. He had crossed Jonson's hand with gold, for one, for private pageants to impress royalty with.

'Resurrection is a matter of faith, Mr Palmer, not money.'

Palmer was tempted to argue the contrary, from ancient tales of chantries, of their masses for the dead, of indulgences, all of it money down in payment to assist the life everlasting.

'You will think about it?' he said instead.

Shakespeare cast his mind back to when he had first met this man. It was in the wake of a payment for the resurrection of an old, dangerous play.

It had not turned out well. He made his excuses and left Palmer where he was.

A strange, ethereal music floated over the audience and into Palmer's ears as if in another time and certainly in another place.

It was emanating from the gallery above the stage in the open-air theatre, crowded out in a special atmosphere of excitement for a new play after the time of plague. Palmer strained to hear, recorders in octaves above other instruments intending to represent the harmony of the universe.

The sounds ran in counterpoint to what was going on among the groundlings on the floor of the Globe. They were a part rapt, part restless crowd of hoi polloi, cap-wearing apprentices jostling the stained jerkins and drab dresses of the older folk. It was coming to the end of the afternoon's play-time after the customary two o'clock start.

How did they get the time off work?

Palmer looked around him up in the galleries, at the more prosperous middling class in sober suits and the wives, plenty out on their own, in whiter, cleaner caps and kerchiefs than the women down below. The finest sort, the gentlemen, in the main unaccompanied, smoked as they looked on from their private 'room' or sat on the fringes of the stage, as much part of the scene as the actors, there to be seen as well as to see and hear.

Onstage, the figure of Pericles, entranced, lay down to sleep.

As in a vision, the goddess Diana appeared above him in the gallery where the musicians were playing, her robes, lit from behind creating an otherworldly impression. She summoned Pericles in an adolescent tenor to her temple in Ephesus. There his lost wife revealed herself, as a priestess of the goddess. The recognition scene was a touching one, reuniting husband, wife and daughter despite it being man, youth and boy.

It was almost too much for Pericles.

No more you gods! Your present kindness makes my past miseries sports.

The man next to Palmer sobbed at Pericles' words. Palmer expected it of the women in the crowd, but a senior official of the Chief Minister? A Whitehall man?

The play ended. This time there was no vulgar jig of song and dance to come – a sign of new times and a new style? Palmer dug the old official in the ribs.

'We'll catch him in the tiring house behind the stage,' he said, 'just follow me, and don't get lost!'

Palmer's badge of office silenced any objections on their way backstage. Inside a confusion of bodies was moving properties, taking off and storing costumes, washing up, getting ready to go out front – every action in its appointed place but entirely random to the uninformed eye. Only the noise and the sweaty smell of men making money from play were commonplace.

Palmer saw Shakespeare talking to Richard Burbage, his Pericles. He interrupted them. Burbage adroitly withdrew.

Palmer introduced the old official. To his embarrassment, the man appeared overcome, too shy to speak beyond a half-suffocated...

'Oh, Mr Shakespeare!'

An awkward silence fell between them as Shakespeare waited for someone to speak. Palmer waited too, but the old official appeared to know no way of asking whatever it was he wanted on behalf of the Chief Minister.

'With *Pericles* launched, we hope you will have more time for other ideas,' Palmer said, to set the ball rolling.

It seemed to wake the old official up. He spoke.

'The Chief Minister is most interested in the possibility of another subject from Plutarch.'

Shakespeare's eyes glinted.

'There are many to choose from,' he said.

'*Timon of Athens*, that's what we mean,' Palmer said, leaving no time to be wasted.

'Mr Palmer knows,' Shakespeare began saying to the official, 'that *Timon* has been set aside. I should be happy to assist the Lord Treasurer in any way I can, except with *Timon*.'

The official's hands fretted anxiously.

'You are sure of that, Mr Shakespeare?'

'I am sure.'

'And nothing will change your mind, nothing *pecuniary*?'

Shakespeare laughed, without the whoop this time.

'Not even that. Now if his lordship has a taste for this *Pericles*, or the Egyptian play...'

'Is there anything else you are working on?' the official asked in desperation, keen to take back something which might serve his master's purpose.

'Nothing in the manner of *Timon*,' Shakespeare said.

~ 13 ~

THE KNOCK on the door of the chamber in the large Stratford house was urgent and repeated.

'Doctor, Dr Hall,' it repeated until the good man roused himself from the bed he shared with his wife Susanna.

She woke too, looking instinctively towards the cradle where their tiny daughter was sleeping.

Hall went to the door. As a doctor, he was used to midnight alarms. He opened the door to see the maidservant standing there.

'There's word from Henley Street, Doctor. Old Mother Shakespeare, she's bad, yow're to come at once.'

The Doctor turned towards his wife.

'Stay here with Elizabeth,' he said.

'Look after the baby,' Susanna commanded the maidservant. 'I'm coming with yow,' she told her husband.

They made their way from New Place and its street of high, prosperous houses, past the town cross and into a street of humbler dwellings. In the old family home in Henley street, they found the family up and waiting.

'She's calling for the priest,' Susanna's aunt Joan said who lived in the same place with her own young family.

Everyone knew what that meant, not the Vicar, but whichever priest of the old faith could be found under cover of darkness if there was one hidden in or near the town. She was baptised in the ancient faith and married in it, old Mary had said often enough, and she would die in it too.

Dr Hall sighed, a sigh that said 'not wise, do not do it'.

'Is there a priest in town?' Susanna asked.

Dr Hall sighed once more but did not argue.

The Shakespeares, like the town, were divided. As for Susanna herself and one of her brothers, their absence from church had been noticed and brought to the attention of the church court. He'd had his work cut out to make her conform. He was a man of the new way, it pleased him to think. As a doctor, he had little truck with the old superstitions and as for politics, every regard for the power of the authorities and the harm they could inflict on the unwise and unwary.

Aunt Joan despatched her husband in search.

Dr Hall climbed his way up the stairs into the old family bedchamber. The old woman was barely visible under the covers of the bed. Her breathing was shallow. He put a hand to her forehead. There was no fever. She was dying of old age.

'Is that yow, John?'

He hesitated to answer – John had been the name of her husband, dead these seven years. The good Doctor knew how the aged lived more in the past than the present.

'John Hall,' he said after a little time, 'Susanna's husband.'

'I know who yow are,' the old woman said, a touch of anger in her voice. 'Yow can do nothing for me – I want the priest, a proper one, mind!'

Dr Hall could not answer her.

'Aunt Joan's man has gone looking for one.' Susanna Hall spoke from the top of the stairs.

'Tell the boy to get … he knows what,' old Mary commanded.

The boy was her term for Richard, the last of the Shakespeare brothers left at home, the one so unlike the others that some said he was one loaf short of the batch. Susanna went back downstairs. A little while after, Dr Hall heard the sound of knocking in the roof along and above from where he stood, in the loft. Susanna Hall came back clutching a mildewed old paper.

By the light of a flickering candle, Dr Hall cast his eye over it and then looked away.

'I haven't seen this,' he said with disgust.

He knew what it was, he'd heard rumours of such things. It was a Catholic testament distributed by underground Jesuits. It claimed to give extreme unction – some called it the last rites – in the absence of a priest.

Susanna gave it to her grandmother.

The old woman sighed with satisfaction as she clutched it in her hands. It did not matter she couldn't read it, now or ever, its presence was enough. Soon she appeared to be sleeping. The cover on the bed barely rose and fell. Then it lay still.

Susanna gave out a sudden sob before recovering herself immediately. There was work to do preparing the old woman for her burial.

'We remember our friend and colleague William Sly.'

The voice of sombre respect belonged to Cuthbert Burbage, speaking among the senior men of the acting company gathered in the Blackfriars Theatre in the dog days of August. The King's Men were back in possession of the playhouse. They were meeting to discuss what to do with it.

Heads bowed – Sly had been in the business as long as anyone could remember. Most of them had been to his funeral, all except William Shakespeare.

'Now to business,' Cuthbert Burbage said. 'First, any news from Will?'

John Hemmings cleared his throat to answer.

'His mother Mary died and was buried...'

'She was a good age,' someone said.

'Yes, yes, three score and ten or more I should think,' Hemmings said, keen to get on. 'So he's still in Stratford. And given that the plague's come back to us here in London, what with the growing number of cases – again! – Will says he sees no pressing reason to return, what with our playhouses closed...'

'But is he writing?' Richard Burbage asked. 'We have to think ahead. We are gathered today to consider what we can do here in the Blackfriars and for the Court season, if the plague relents.'

They wished the wretched disease would make up its mind instead of this up-down-up pattern.

'We will have to close the Globe up anyway,' his brother said.

Other voices muttered agreement. It was what the company did as autumn approached. The Globe stayed closed in winter, unrented out to the amazement of the other playhouse landlords in the capital. But then, the King's Men were actor-owners, company and playhouse, another inexplicable rarity in the normal way of doing things.

'And go out on tour?' Hemmings asked.

This was also usual, albeit the older men were more settled in their ways these days and sent the younger ones out. After all, the King offered compensation when plague closed the theatres, and twice the fees the old Queen had for Court performances over Christmas.

'Looks like it,' said Cuthbert Burbage, 'towards Marlborough and then Coventry.'

The news pleased Hemmings. It was not so far from his old home town. He might just go along with the youngsters and make a right royal return there for a few days, swagger about as 'boy done well'. Was he Droitwich's most famous son these days? Actor or not, he liked to think so.

'But is Will *writing*?' Richard Burbage persisted in asking, knowing where his bread was best baked when it came to writers.

'I'm not sure,' Hemmings admitted. 'He is busy with family matters – he has a new granddaughter, remember, and his mother's just died. He says there's also been some family trouble with the consistory court. Something about his brother and sister being hauled up "for the customary reason".'

'What, Shakespeare's in the bawdy court?' a voice called out, laughing.

It was the popular name given to church courts, showing what much of their business was about – cases of sexual misbehaviour. But a brother and sister?

Hemmings attempted to look severe.

'More likely to do with church attendance,' he said, knowing the Shakespeare family record. 'But he did mention a subject which is interesting him...'

The attention to him grew sharper.

'... it's complicated to explain.'

'When isn't it, with Will's plots!'

The offending voice was quickly silenced.

'What I gather is this,' Hemmings said. 'The heart of the story is the separation of husband and wife and a bet on the spotlessness of her honour in his absence.'

'We've heard that one before,' the offending voice insisted.' Since when was Will so keen on female virtue?

Hemmings ignored it.

'The *colour* of the piece sounds promising. It involves relations between the old British kings – *Cymbeline*'s his title for the work – *and* the Romans, who are very much in fashion as we know in these imperial times. He expects the story to journey from land to land. He says he sees scope for music, dancing and the use of modern theatre machinery.'

Good for the Blackfriars and its aim to attract a smarter, richer audience, everyone realised, good too for any season at Court and not at all bad for the old Globe itself, next year, if the play was written on a grand enough scale; and if the wretched plague relented.

'Very much in the romance style,' Cuthbert Burbage said.

'Like *Pericles*,' his brother suggested.

'Talking of which, has everybody heard?'

Everybody had. The embittered George Wilkins had got round their ploy of having the play *Pericles* registered for publication by Ned Blount. He had written his own version, in novella fashion – in prose for heaven's sake! – published by a rival of Blount's, one Henry Gosson.

'The cheek of it – he follows *our* plotline. He doesn't dare use his own ideas for the fate of the princess...'

'... which just goes to show that he is playing off *our* success...'

'... *and* Will's reputation.'

'However did it get past the censor?'

The same question was exercising Richard Palmer after he heard about it from his snout inside the printers' guild. The answer he got, piecing a number of answers together, was that it had fallen between several stools.

'It is not in play form,' Buc told him, 'therefore it is beyond our authority.'

For the time being, he thought to himself.

It fell towards the Bishop of London's man, but the word was that such fanciful works of fiction only briefly detained that censor. The same was true of the Stationers' company whose attitude – publish wherever possible – was prompted by their members' interests.

It was not a happy state of affairs, as Richard Palmer said to the Chief Minister's official.

'I must say, you appear to have some animus over this business,' the Whitehall man said, whose cousin was the Bishop's censor.

Palmer did. Wilkins had stolen a march on everyone. Palmer had not forgotten Ellen and her fate at his hands.

'The man's an animal,' he said.

The old official blinked. Since Palmer was one himself, this Wilkins must be extremely odious. And since when did good morals make a writer, no more than they made a good politician, or – dare he think it – ruler of a nation?

Palmer made a point of seeking out John Hemmings.

'Don't accuse *us*,' the old actor said. 'We're as upset as you are, and for good reason. *Pericles* is still fresh on the stage. We want folk coming to the play, not reading the book!'

As to why Palmer was annoyed, Hemmings couldn't fathom. The mystery only deepened when Palmer demanded that the King's Men never use Wilkins again.

'We're not going to,' Hemmings protested, 'not after what he's just done to us!'

'Let me tell you this,' Palmer warned him. 'Nothing for the stage by George Wilkins is *ever* going to get past the censor.'

That, thought Hemmings, was taking it too far.

Palmer made Wilkins his business elsewhere. He went to see Wilkins's publisher, Henry Gosson, who was unhelpful. Later, Gosson warned Wilkins that he had a new enemy.

'Richard Palmer?' Wilkins sneered. 'The man's a hypocrite and a lightweight!'

'He works for Tilney and Buc,' Gosson warned him.

'That's as may be. He can work for the man in the moon as far as I'm concerned. Don't worry, I have the measure of Mr Palmer!'

News of Palmer's adventures got back to Sir George Buc. It troubled him.

For all that he had said to Gosson, they troubled George Wilkins too, in a different way. He waited for Palmer outside in the road, one night when Palmer was making his way home.

'I want a word with you!' Wilkins said.

Palmer walked on.

'What did you do with that girl of mine you took away?' Wilkins shouted after him.

Palmer stopped in his tracks and walked back towards the speaker. He cast his eyes around carefully. No, it was just

Wilkins; and Wilkins wouldn't touch an officer of the King, would he? An itchy part of Palmer hoped that he might, the part that knew where his knife was, the one he carried in a panel on the inside of his boot. Wilkins might have the bigger fists, but a blade made all men equal.

Up close to Wilkins, he spoke.

'The girl you beat, the one carrying a child?'

'The one you took away and was never seen again,' Wilkins said. 'Listen, you make trouble for me and I'll do the same for you. I know how you've been interesting yourself in my writings.'

'Good, because they are never going to see the light of day, not as far as I'm concerned!'

'Is that in your power, Palmer, is it really?'

Palmer winked at him and ducked his head suggestively. Wilkins's fist clenched. And then unclenched. He watched Palmer walk away from him.

'I am hearing complaints from all sorts of people about you,' Buc said when he called Palmer in to see him.

'If it's about George Wilkins…'

'It is … and it isn't. About the man himself, I care nothing. About the power you are accused of claiming as your own, I care a great deal. That power is mine.'

Palmer nodded. He had, he knew, no defence.

'It's a personal matter…' he started to say, quickly realising that this only made it worse.

'Just so,' Buc said, 'and so it should remain. It has nothing to do with your work.'

'I am sorry,' Palmer said.

'So you ought to be. I have had Master Gosson telling me he'll be seeking to publish a version of the play itself, no doubt advised by our friend, and he hopes that I, not you will be the one to look at it. As I shall. I have also had a letter from Mr Shakespeare.'

The name made Palmer look up sharply. What had he got to complain about?

'Mr Shakespeare expresses his fear, and the fears of his *King's* Men, that it is your actions which have brought on what Gosson intends to do in publishing the play, which acts against what has already been agreed by them with Master Blount. I think we would agree, Mr Palmer, that Blount is the better publisher for *Pericles*, in all our interests?'

The best of a bad bunch in his opinion, Palmer kept to himself. He heard his sentence out.

'I must warn you to act in future with the greatest care in the execution of your duties. I am aware that it was the Chief Minister who recommended you, but I am sure he would be the first to say that your duty is to act in the interest of the Law, the State and the Crown, and not on the basis of what the Italians call the Vendetta.'

No, revenge was not in the manual of the perfect courtier, Palmer bet.

Nor was it in the manner of William Shakespeare, he thought to himself afterwards in the street. The man was wedded to caution, especially since his brush with fate during the Essex business seven years ago.

Another thought nagged Palmer. Wasn't Shakespeare away in Stratford? The letter of complaint must have been a put up job. He knew just who by.

Hemmings was uncontrite when Palmer found him in the familiar alehouse on Bankside.

'I think you should be very careful,' Hemmings said. 'I have only to say the word.'

He had friends around him was his point. Palmer could not miss them, scattered among the crowd of drinkers. They were the ones keeping an obvious ear out to what was going on between their colleague and this unwelcome stranger.

'Using Shakespeare to make a petty complaint...' Palmer started to say.

'The complaint was not petty. As for William's making it, Sir George has a great appreciation of the wordsmith, more than he does your man of business. Sir George is quite the patron, a would-be writer too by all accounts. Quite the brother-in-arms for those of the quillpen fraternity!'

'So Wilkins is the victim to be defended by all!'

'Look, Palmer,' Hemmings said, leaning forward and lowering his voice, 'what is it you have against George Wilkins? He's a rogue, I agree, a beast too, but there are plenty of those in our business and in yours. What is so special about Wilkins?'

Palmer leaned forward.

'This is my story,' he said.

Was it wise? More to the point, what was the point? Nonetheless he found himself telling it.

'There was a young girl, not a maiden as your stories demand, a serving girl, not a princess.'

Hemmings tapped his fingers on his pot of beer impatiently. Palmer was not to be hurried.

'One man, her master, used her. She had a child and was
rescued. Then another man – a regular Mr Vice out of your old
morality tale – he used her too, only he made promises of a
better life, a life to which she followed him. She was discarded.
Soon she's in the brothel, a real one, not one where virgin
virtue shines out to God and beckons all his ministering angels
to protect her. The bawd beats her. One day, he beats her – her
and her unborn child – to death.'

'I see,' said Hemmings who had heard as bad in his time.
'And the murderer is Wilkins?'

Palmer made no sign.

'And no-one took him before the Law?'

'His tracks were covered by circumstance.'

'A sad tale, commonplace too,' Hemmings said.

'The second man in the story was one of your kind, an
actor.'

'You surprise me.'

Hemmings did not look surprised.

'No,' Palmer said, 'not a story as would interest your
playhouse crowd, those in front of the stage or those on it.'

'And you are a man of iron virtue?'

Palmer thought back to the room upstairs where Wilkins
plied his real trade. No, his virtue was as pliable as the rest's, in
some things. He sinned, but he was not evil – that was the
difference. Wilkins was evil. As for the players, he realised that
they were bound to defend one of their own so what Hemmings
said next came as a surprise.

'Mr Palmer, such as Wilkins, they get their payback in the
end even if they don't get it at our hands. We won't work with
him again. I can't speak for the others except to say that he had
one shortcoming above all the others you lay before me.'

'And what is that?'

'He cannot write.'

The seasons changed, the plague in London did not.

There were no plays in the capital. The younger actors stayed alive by setting out on the road to earn their keep on tour, going from town to town on foot with tabor and fife, seeking welcome and a recognition of their licence to perform. Some town fathers granted it willingly, others paid the actors off, depending on the severity of the religion informing the politics of the place and their respect – or not – for the name of the King whose men the licence said these players were. One or two towns were bold enough to send the players on their way penniless.

Their chief writer Shakespeare stayed at home in Stratford. His acting days were long over. He had no function in a travelling company doing a *Pericles* out of place and without its special effects. There was an only granddaughter to watch over and a family to enjoy at last. With the death of his mother, he was head of the family, out on his own, next in line for the grim reaper. The thought did not detain him, nor would it leave him.

His *Cymbeline* drew him more and more into it. It never seemed to end, because he did not want it to. He sat in his orchard, the trees burdened with autumn fruit, early windfall spotting the ground – from old habits he knew he would pick up the fallen fruit once he was ready to go indoors. Leaves above shaded him from the fading heat of a season soon to pass into winter.

> *Fear no more the heat of the sun,*
> *Nor the furious winter's rages;*

Thou thy worldly task has done
Home art gone, and ta'en thy wages.

The words looked right enough to him on the sheet –
requiem for a dead boy, not dead and in fact a girl, a princess,
shortly to revive. He spoke them out loud. Good. Music would
round them out perfectly. The King's Men had taken on the
excellent consort of players previously employed by the
children's company at the Blackfriars playhouse. Everything at
the Blackfriars was going to be better all round, for the
company and for its chief writer.

Out of turn, his mind lurched back to a memory
suppressed. There was no face to it, to his own dead boy. How
long had it been, how many years since the lad was put under
the ground? A dozen years? Really?

With his pen on the parchment in front of him he could
bring souls back from the seeming dead, Lazarus-like. There
was something childish in this, as if, for a moment, he could
change life and death and alter it to a new reality. In such a
moment, his faceless boy lived.

But when he put the pen down, and when he went back
into the house behind him and into its present world, this
power vanished, into air.

As October passed by, word came that the plague had abated in
London sufficiently for plays to be wanted in the Court's
Christmas festivities. *Pericles* refloated would require the
presence of its author and stager. Once more, the Stratford

family would have to do without their head in the season of the year at midwinter.

Back in London, Shakespeare stayed in the room on Bankside where his brother had died exactly a year before, after Christmas. He visited the grave in St Saviour's Church. He spoke to his departed brother inside the safety of his mind.

'Mother is with you, if what priests teach us is to be believed. Your son too – since babes have souls. Was yours baptised? You never said, I never asked.'

What other news was there to tell?

'Susanna has her child, a daughter Elizabeth. Your Aunt Joan's brood is growing up, my wife Anne has found the will to live now she has a grandchild to fuss over. Your brothers ... well, they never change!'

There was no answer. What did he expect?

'The plague is still with us, as it has been for half our lives. We work at what we can.'

How long must I continue? How long, Oh Lord, how long?

'It's another five, six years until my half century. How many of our acting sort beat that mark?'

Edmund hadn't, little more than half that number.

'... and I am left to count the days.'

He stood as if waiting for some response.

There was other business to be done, he told himself at last.

He turned away to put the cold stone grave behind him, walking out into the wintry air. The Trojan play, offspring of the terrible time when Lord Essex revolted against the old Queen was being sought by a publisher. It was owned by the King's Men, but they had asked him if it could go in order to put some money into the company coffers after a plague-riddled year.

'One for the bookish,' Cuthbert Burbage said, 'it never made its name on the stage.'

Truth was they had barely tried it, Shakespeare protested to himself as he walked west towards the Globe. It had been of its time and was therefore now out of it. Let it go. Should they do the same with *Timon*? No, he would not let that one go, not yet whatever he said to the contrary.

Maybe one day someone else could make it work where Middleton and he had failed.

It was the Trojan play which drew Palmer's attention when he was visiting the works of its printer in the course of his duties.

'They still can't have enough of him,' the printer said, 'even this,' he added, showing Palmer the freshly printed title page of *Troilus & Cressida*, on it the name of its author, William Shakespeare, because it was a name that sold.

Palmer recalled a bitter conversation on horseback on the road from Stratford, about Achilles the coward, Ulysses the liar, old Nestor the windbag and Helen the slut, these so-called immortals rendered as they really were in the eyes of a writer who had seen their sort close to.

'And sonnets, Master Elde?' Palmer asked the printer.

'Those were the days!' the printer laughed, thinking back to the decade before when sonnets were all the rage. 'You never know. People still call for his *Venus* and we printers still print it. Ah now, to find a store of sonnets, that would be something.'

Palmer had that store, in his chamber.

'Would fifty serve?' Palmer asked.

'Mr Palmer, you are pulling my leg!'

'A hundred? A hundred and fifty?'

'A treasure trove, Mr Palmer!' the printer exclaimed, entering into the spirit of the game. 'Tell you what, Mr Palmer, you ever find the man as has 'em, you introduce him to me!'

Beyond the inky world of books and printers, the world span a little smaller for Buc's man, as Palmer was becoming known, when he heard news of a noble marriage. His informant was the reliable Chief Minister's official.

'Lady Cumberland's daughter, my Lady Anne Clifford, has become the Countess of Dorset.'

A large fish landed by a tiny girl, Palmer thought, recalling his one sight of her with Emilia Lanier on the road outside Henley when he was chasing the Gunpowder men. He hoped that the new Countess would be better in bed and at board, as the prayerbook invoked, than her saintly mother had likely been.

Emilia would be pleased. Or would she? Hadn't the old official once told him that marriage of the daughter would mean the loss of the mother's home? Lady Cumberland and her waiting woman Emilia would be out on their ear.

If the sonnets held value enough for Emilia to ask to buy hers back a few months ago, how much more so now, now that she was out on the loose?

~ 14 ~

THE SUMMONS from Tilney was unexpected.

The old man was looking more overblown than ever. He was still recovering from his winter's duties for the Court.

'I shall not be holding readings of new plays for the summer season,' he announced to Palmer.

It was no surprise. The plague had not disappeared with the winter as it most often did. The playhouses were likely to remain closed.

'... so I have no use for your services.'

Tilney spoke with a deliberate finality.

Palmer was staggered.

'I thought Buc...' he began to say.

'Buc may have used you,' the old man sniffed, 'but it's my office pays you. I *am* still the Master of the Revels. And by the way, Buc doesn't want you either so it's no use applying to him – you upset him over the Wilkins business. He gives, I must say, a higher value to the opinion of Mr Shakespeare and his kind than to you, or indeed to me! But there we are, Buc is the man for our new age, or so I am told!'

There was no use arguing, Palmer realised at once, a judgement supported by the sight of a purse dangling in his master's hand to pay him off. Old instincts, to take the money and run pressed Palmer forward to accept it.

Leaving Tilney, he went to find the Chief Minister's old official in the palace at Whitehall. The man was sympathetic, but there was no chance of an interview with his master, he said, and no known business going for Palmer.

'My Lord Salisbury and I, we are working on his great contract for the King.'

And what was that, Palmer asked to be reminded? The official was too proud of it to keep it entirely quiet. Palmer soon understood that the deal was to pay off the royal debt and to grant the King an annual income provided he surrendered his own tax-raising powers. The sums mentioned were enormous, hundreds of thousands of pounds, the income of several kingdoms. It was a price way beyond Palmer's imagination or the little purse of silver nestling inside his clothes.

'Do you think that will work?' he asked, artlessly.

He knew what he would do if he were the monarch, take the debt resolution and hold on to his prerogatives regardless!

The official appeared hurt.

'We shall bear you in mind,' he said, as kindly as he could.

Palmer made his way back by river to the old city, and into his favourite watering hole, the Bell Inn in Carter Lane.

Three pots of beer did not enlighten him any further about his future. He was not without money, in his purse or with the goldsmith off Cheapside. But the prospect of a return to his old business no longer appealed to him. He knew the risk, that he would run his money down and then be left with nothing. That, for once, he had to avoid; he was not getting any younger.

He wandered the streets around Blackfriars. A sound, of music, was coming from inside the playhouse there. The actors would not yet know about his dismissal. What could they be working on? What would be the point with the playhouses shut for Lent and the Court festivities over?

Palmer decided to go in for one last time. If he found Shakespeare there, he would settle with him once and for all.

Fear no more the heat of the sun.

A young man was chanting rather than singing it. He broke off when he spotted Palmer.

It was an older man, Hemmings who approached the intruder.

'We are rehearsing, Mr Palmer. Mr Shakespeare's new play.'

'There's not much call for plays in plague time,' Palmer said.

'There is away from London. We are going out on tour, around the eastern coast and further inland.'

Palmer asked him where.

'Ipswich, Hythe, New Romney. We shall travel by sea. We may be away the entire summer. There is a further call for us in the Midlands and over towards the borders with Wales.'

So the Globe was likely to remain closed all year, and the Blackfriars out of use other than for rehearsals like this one under its protecting roof. It was no longer of interest to him, Palmer reminded himself. He knew what was.

'So where is he?'

There was no use Hemmings pretending not to understand who was meant.

'Mr Shakespeare is still in the country, in Stratford. He will probably summer there.'

Better that he did, Hemmings reckoned, than upset himself with the 'waste', as Shakespeare had put it to him, of his *Cymbeline* coming to the stage not in London but on tour. It was a Court play, everyone accepted, a Blackfriars play, a

London one. Justice could not be done to it out in the country with a travelling company and no special effects.

'I have news,' Palmer said, and told Hemmings of his dismissal.

Hemmings's reaction was predictable.

'We are very sorry to hear it.'

The words did not match his eyes which flashed amusement.

Palmer had nothing to stay for. He made his way home. Passing Wilkins's establishment on the corner of his street, he heard, from noise inside, that Wilkins was still in business.

What had he achieved, Palmer asked himself, listening to the usual tavern sounds? Wilkins went scot-free. His writings had been stopped but even that was unsure with Palmer out of the way, sacked from the one place where he could do the man most harm.

He was not in the best frame of mind when he reached his chamber. He sat on his bed, his ark, the one remnant of the Palmer family past and its former prosperity. Other than his money, what did he have? An old thought pestered its way into his mind. He reached for the compartment under his bed. He took out the papers inside and laid them out on his bed.

George Elde the printer was astonished as he looked the through the sonnets.

'You weren't pulling my leg, Mr Palmer,' he said. 'There's a hundred and fifty or so by my count. What are they all about?'

Palmer pretended ignorance.

He had revisited the story the night before, of the older man, the praise-singer hired to bid a young man marry and have children, and their metamorphosis into something far more emotive. It brought back memories of first discovery, when he was sent on an ever-increasing trail of sonnets by the Chief Minister, Palmer's first case for him in the days after the Essex uprising.

From fairest creatures we desire increase.

He had shut his mind to the dried bloodstain and found once again the point where the sonnets turned personal, when any child of the poet's muse should be conceived...

... for love of me.

For love of him! The claim still had the power to astonish, of this humble-born, William Shakespeare bidding the high-born, Henry, Earl of Southampton to honour the bond between them in such a way.

The flavours of the poetry had lost nothing of their intensity, of the sort a man might send a mistress. Absence made the heart grow fonder and more bitter, jealous even, themes worked out in clusters of sonnets, matter too good just to waste on one. Were some unsent?

The dark woman, Emilia, had appeared again.

Two loves I have of comfort and despair......
My better angel is a man right fair,
My worser spirit a woman coloured ill.

The boy-muse stole her or was stolen by her, did it matter which? The poet's witty loveplay with her turned sour until his final, acid fulmination on the curse of lust...

... past reason hunted, and no sooner had past reason hated.

She disappeared from sight.

Palmer knew why – Emilia's inconvenient conception of her bastard child and her ejection from the golden half-world she had inhabited carrying a child she liked to think had noble blood from one Henry or another when in fact it was more likely the actor's parting shot.

'Are they of interest to you?' Palmer asked the printer.

Elde raised an eyebrow.

'I hope I'll get to print them,' he said, 'but we'll need a publisher to put up the money and to sell them, someone ambitious, prepared to take risks. I take it you do not have the permission of the author?'

The risks were personal as well as financial, Elde meant. From brief sight of the content, and given their number he knew that these were not commonplace froth. As poetry went, this could be big, very big. Shakespeare's *Venus* still sold. But something like these ... who could tell?

'Are they about real people?' Elde asked, wanting to know just what he might be getting himself into.

Palmer spun him a story about poetic imagination before getting to the point.

'Do you have a publisher in mind?'

Elde nodded.

Thomas Thorpe was not the kind of publisher Palmer had expected. His opinion of the man was not improved on second meeting.

'Sonnets ... sonnets,' Thorpe said, his eyes darting everywhere, away from the man before him. 'A fashion of the eighties and nineties. We were knee-deep in sonnets, *then*.'

Palmer did not take the bait. His own eyes were wandering too, around the books on Thorpe's shelves. They reminded him that the man did a line in Ben Jonson, including the arse-numbing masque of Palmer's buttock memory. Anyone who published Jonson took risks, if the bruiser's reputation over his business dealings were half true.

'And how ... how...'

'How did I acquire them?' Palmer cut in. 'They came to me in my former work, not directly – it was not a matter for the Revels office since poetry isn't its business. Let us say, the man who owned them wanted an opinion, about their quality and about their...'

'Price?'

'Just so.'

'And who ... who...'

'Who might this man be?'

Palmer had already decided on his anwer. He would use one of his aliases. William Henry would be revived as...

'... Mr W.H., that is how he wishes to be known to anyone beyond me. He is, shall we say, setting out for pastures new and so he is turning into cash such property as he has.'

It wasn't a bad summary of the position Palmer might be in himself. If Thorpe smelled Catholic mystery, so be it, he reckoned privately. The man had form himself, with Jesuits in Madrid when England and Spain were still at war. Might it even make him more understanding?

For the first time Thorpe's eyes stilled and focused on the man in front of him. They appeared to sense the opportunity. The Shakespeare name sold. Thorpe had a copy of an early story-poem of the writer's, apprentice work not worth publishing, leastwise not on its own. Why not put the two together? He said as much to Palmer, and its name,

'*A Lover's Complaint*, about a maid seduced.'

It threw Palmer's mind unwillingly towards Ellen, on his bed, bleeding to death. And how would this business of seduction be described in frolicsome verse by Wilkins's writing partner?

He said nothing.

Thorpe was making quick calculations. Shakespeare was out of town for the foreseeable future. His early love poetry had tumbled off the shelves and multiplied in further editions in months. A publisher prepared to act quickly could make a lot of money first and answer questions later. As for the provenance, there were layers of defence – Palmer here in front of him, a hard man to break, he guessed, and behind him a mysterious Mr W.H., mysterious enough for Palmer not to reveal and therefore for the publisher to deny – honestly too – and hide behind. A lot of 'honestly believed' and 'don't knows' would make it difficult for anyone to make a complaint stick.

It was a risk worth taking, Thorpe decided – enter *Shakespeare's Sonnets* for publication together with *A Lover's Complaint* at the Stationer's hall and see what happened. Above all, be prepared to move fast, in the printing and the selling.

Now to money.

'We pay five pounds, six at the most,' Thorpe said, his eyes beginning to dart around again.

Palmer smiled.

'My orders are clear,' he said. 'Not less than twelve. The author is William Shakespeare, in his sonnet springtime. *Venus*,

I am told, is still selling. The sonnets come from the same stable and from the same time.'

Palmer knew they did. The author had once told him as much. They were in tune with those times. But these?

Thorpe's eyes focused once more.

'Twelve pounds, but in two equal payments, one in advance and one on licensed publication.'

Palmer held out his hand. After Thorpe shook it to make the deal, Palmer kept it extended until Thorpe filled it with a bag of money.

~ 15 ~

A FINE MIDSUMMER day several weeks later found Palmer surveying a stall in St Paul's Churchyard. Shakespeare's slim sonnet books were laid out in front of him, on sale for the first time. Elde had printed them as he'd said he would, borne out by his name on the title page. The censor, the clerical cousin of the Chief Minister's old official, had approved them, or rather, had taken the hint sugared by a few silver coins not to look too closely beyond the author's name.

The deal done, the money received in full, Palmer had intended to put as much distance as possible between the publication and himself but today he was in holiday mood. He could not resist asking for a copy to look through. Thorpe had been coy about letting him have one.

'Your Mr W.H. is the man entitled and will be welcome to the usual number, on presenting himself to me.'

Both men knew this would not happen.

Palmer picked up a copy and opened it, ink-on-paper-smelling, straight from the press.

'What the...'

He re-read the title page, his neck prickling with concern. He read the words out, quietly, to himself.

To the only begetter of these ensuing sonnets Mr W.H. all happiness and that eternity promised by our ever-living poet.

A light sweat broke out on his forehead. Thorpe had pulled a fast one! He had put the name of the procurer into a dedication in order to cover himself in case of any comeback from the authorities.

'Ask Mr William Henry,' he could hear Thorpe saying. Who's he? 'Ask Mr Palmer, he knows him.'

He would cross that bridge when it came to it, Palmer decided. There were plenty of other Mr W.H.s who could be thrown up as a smokescreen, the plays-mad William Herbert, Earl of Pembroke for one, a rising young man at Court. Ah, but Thorpe would soon squeal more accurately, depending on who asked him. It might be time to lie low for a while, Palmer told himself. Oxford at Christmas?

'Will you take it, sir?' the bookseller asked. 'Into the heart of our loving Mr Shakespeare and all for a shilling!'

'I think not,' Palmer said.

It was too guilty a memento.

A purchaser of the book pressed it down on the table in the alehouse in front of John Hemmings, forcing the actor to look up. Hemmings was startled by whom he saw. The man standing in front of him was the Right Honourable Henry Wriothesley, third Earl of Southampton, Knight of the Garter and Master of the Queen's Horse.

'My Lord!' Hemmings stammered, getting to his feet.

It was nearly ten years since the actor had seen the noble lord close to, when he visited the Globe in his time of disfavour and exclusion from Court under the old Queen. It was fifteen since the days of intimacy between the young man and their playwright Shakespeare. Southampton's star had crashed, fatally or so it seemed after his involvement in the Essex business. Then it had risen again, like a phoenix under King James – that much the actors had seen from a respectful distance whenever they played at Court. He was a fabulous bird but one who no longer cast his eye on their doings or his wings over their fortunes.

Until now.

'How?' Southampton demanded.

Hemmings knew what he meant, about the publication of sonnets in which the noble lord played the principal character, the poet's fair young friend, his muse. His high tenor voice had lost none of its arrogance, or his green-grey eyes their foxy intelligence.

Hemmings thumbed through the book. Truth was he did not know how and Shakespeare was away in Stratford, unable to tell him. Hemmings had been left to do the company's 'business as usual' in the capital, still worried by the plague, while their younger men strutted the provinces earning their keep in these difficult times.

The dedication to Mr W.H. was a clue, but who could that be? The man in front of him, Henry Wriothesley in some game of reversed initials? Then why was he here complaining? Hemmings's thoughts grasped wildly at 'Mr William Himself.' Only William was not the sort to be so rash.

He was confused. He said as much to Southampton.

'I shall want an explanation from Mr Shakespeare himself...' was what he got back.

So the days of 'Will' were past.

'... because this little book will cause me *great* embarrassment.'

It was an embarrassment reduced since Southampton had taken the precaution of having his steward buy up and destroy all the available copies not yet sold. He gave Hemmings a long, hard look and then turned on his elegant heel and left.

He was a leading figure at Court, Hemmings did not need to be reminded. True to form, the lord's famous temper had managed to put that position at risk more than once, and his face and figure, handsome for a man in his mid-thirties, were no longer as fresh as the King liked. But he was close to Queen Anne. A great landowner, he was also a leading investor in what was the talk of the City harbourside, the present expedition to the Americas. He was not a man to be annoyed at any level, Hemmings reminded himself. He had influence enough and plenty of ready money...

... and he had too much at stake in the courtly dance of politics.

Southampton was, rumour whispered, dancing deft attendance on the King. James and his entourage were to be invited to the Earl's home in Hampshire for a right royal entertainment intended as a gesture of manifest allegiance from a man once accused of high treason. Any awkward embarrassment, especially one which might trip up the neatest foot, was unwelcome. Sonnets hinting at his own private business, so long in the past as it was, his *unreliable* past, qualified as such an embarrassment, that much was clear.

Hemmings watched him go. He could not ignore the visit. Nobles did not condescend into common alehouses unless the matter was exceptional.

A letter from Hemmings covering a copy of the sonnets book sent Shakespeare packing for an early return to London. His wife Anne got no sensible explanation from him. His daughter

Susanna fared little better. Only to his son-in-law did Shakespeare explain.

'Lord Southampton is angry.'

'Does that matter to you?' Dr Hall asked.

It would have once, the older man reflected, personally. Now it was a matter of policy.

'He is intimate with Their Majesties, I am a King's Man. It pays to stay out of trouble with the high and mighty. Hemmings thinks that too, so it is a company matter as well.'

'How did this come about?' Hall asked, examining the publication.

'Palmer,' Shakespeare said.

Hall knew him – the Chief Minister's agent who had come after his father-in-law in the wake of the uprising which had seen Southampton implicated as a prime mover. The man Palmer suffered from an interesting medical condition which Hall had successfully treated. He knew the man's body better than his mind.

'How do you know?' he asked, handing the book back, unexamined, to his father-in-law.

'He confiscated my originals. He never returned them. As for the procurer identified in the dedication, Mr W.H., it's an alias I have known him use. It can be nobody else.'

'What will you do?'

Shakespeare stood up from his packing.

'See the publisher, see the Master of the Revels, see ... Southampton.'

'How long has it been, Will?'

The man standing in front of him was known and yet unknown.

To me, fair friend, you never can be old.

Yes, it was the same golden boy he once wrote about, Shakespeare told himself. Equally he could be any other toughened by the exigencies of time, hardened like a willowy sapling grown thicker round the trunk with maturing age. The boy could be his own father now that the bloom of youth was gone. Time had passed since the airless room in the Tower and the deal to ensure Southampton's survival, landless, imprisoned; eight years ago, nearly nine.

Frightening Thorpe with his knowledge of the identity of Mr W.H. had not been difficult. Reassuring Tilney had been more so. Most difficult of all was this meeting.

'Thorpe will not reprint whatever the demand,' Shakespeare said by way of compensation.

The understanding had not been easy.

'I acquired the work in good faith, Mr Shakespeare.'

'From one Richard Palmer who also works under the name of William Henry. Do you deny it?'

Thorpe made no answer.

'... he has no *title* to them.'

This word had not alarmed the publisher. Title was not something the Law was interested in, not in the matter of books.

'He got them,' Shakespeare told him, 'not on his own account but on the Government's.'

The G-word had a greater effect.

'So are you saying they are stolen goods?'

Thorpe had always assumed that they were, Palmer looked the type.

'... stolen from the Government?' Which was another matter, much more awkward.

'The Government might think so.'

'I see. Then ... then what is it you want from me?'

'You would be wise not to put any more on sale. You would be equally wise not to reprint them.'

'Mr Shakespeare!'

Thorpe was genuinely alarmed.

'... I can't do that. I would be out of pocket...'

... as well as shorn of his profits from the publishing stroke of the century.

'How much?'

Shakespeare watched Thorpe's eyes swivel left and right in response to his question.

'Twenty pounds,' Thorpe said.

'I'll give you ten. I have the money with me. It is all that I can spare in these difficult times.'

Shakespeare put the purse on the table.

Thorpe made some rapid calculations. If he was slow in stopping the call for stock already printed, there was still a profit to be had. The bookseller was already asking for more despite threats from Southampton's steward, for under-the-counter sale.

'And if I don't agree?'

Shakespeare fixed him in the wandering eye.

'There is one who is angrier and more powerful than I am.'

'The damage has already been done,' Southampton said to Shakespeare.

He had read the sonnets, every one. Many he had never seen before, the ones to – what was her name? The dark woman, the old Lord Chamberlain's piece? He couldn't remember. Some of the others, unread before, he found surprising in the anger they aimed at him.

He did not like anyone reading such things. Even the new Queen, who liked to flirt with him since her husband liked flirting elsewhere, who had already read them which was how he had heard of their publication, even her admiration irked him, especially her fascination with male admiring male.

Didn't her husband? Didn't he just!

'What was her name?' Southampton asked Shakespeare, about the dark woman.

'Emilia Bassano, now Lanier.'

'Ah yes, Emilia. A bedmate of the first order – didn't you find so, Will?'

Shakespeare let the remark pass. Southampton was not finished with him.

'Some of these sonnets, they are angry, distempered I'd say.'

Disappointed, Shakespeare thought, despairing even, not intemperate.

' … *a canker in the rose* … *lilies that fester smell far worse than weeds*. Harsh words which I do not remember you ever saying to me, not face to face,' Southampton said.

Sonnets that were not sent.

Shakespeare explained.

'Poetic colour, the working out of images and ideas.'

'Were they really about me?'

'All drama requires circumstance. They were and they were not.'

'So I must live with whatever copies are out in the world,' Southampton said, mentally excluding the majority that he had been able to buy back, 'being pored over by the curious, telling a story which is, and at the same time isn't? Reputation is everything, we are taught.'

Shakespeare did not answer. Characters he had written talked a lot about reputation, most for it, one against. It mattered, he knew. It mattered to him more than it should.

'And this other work, *A Lover's Complaint*, about some country wench let down by a man of rank. Was that really you and I, Will? I never treated you *quite* like that, did I?'

No answer came.

'So, the best that can be said is that no more will follow?' Southampton asked.

'No more.'

'No, no more.'

Emilia Lanier was even angrier.

'Why has he done this to me now?' she shouted at no-one in her empty room, a book of the sonnets she could ill afford in front of her.

There was no Lady Cumberland to turn to or to join with in prayer in the mean little London house in Clerkenwell to which she had returned along with the mean husband. What was the good of prayer in this case anyway? Her anger wanted letting like blood. How else could she express it? Send her husband Lanier to see Palmer again? No, that was useless, *he* was useless.

She would play the man at his own game. She would go back to the idea she had been playing with for years...

~ 16 ~

AUTUMN CAME, this one with a coldness heralding an early winter. The players were glad to be back in full company in London, preparing their Christmas plays for the Court.

Tilney liked the new work they rehearsed before him – *Cymbeline*. So, he was sure, would Their Majesties. He was also pleased that the actors' chief writer was dancing attendance on him. It was good that Mr Shakespeare was no longer indulging in one of his too frequent country absences. There was a time for retirement, to Tilney's mind. It was called the repose of the grave.

Richard Palmer was less busy. He had returned to his old work. Once again the old Alderman wanted his flighty, not-so-young-now wife pursued along with her actor men friends.

'And did they have ... connection?' the old City father liked to ask, saliva creaming his lips.

Tales of thrusting bums and legs splayed wide appeared to do the trick.

After a session in the Bell inn on the proceeds, Palmer wandered home tired. In Clerkenwell he should have been more cautious. A pair of eyes was watching him pass.

He was lying on his bed half asleep when, out of nowhere, his door exploded inwards!

Wilkins stood in the doorway, a second, burly man at his shoulder. A third man guarded their backs in case anyone should be unwise enough to intervene. Palmer instantly knew the feeling of a cornered rat. Imitate the action? He darted low and dived for the exit. Wilkins laughed as he collared him and threw him back into the room.

Wilkins motioned to the other men. The care with which one of them propped the unhinged door against the wall was surprisingly delicate.

Only the first two or three blows hurt Palmer, forcing him to the ground. For the rest he felt nothing, not yet.

'That's for *Pericles*,' Wilkins shouted as he kicked out at the prone man, Palmer's fingers digging at the floorboard where the stain of Ellen's blood darkened the wood. 'And that's for the girl,' Wilkins added, his kick sending stabs of searing pain through the kidneys of his victim.

'Leave him,' Wilkins said after some more of the same.

The second, solicitous man pulled Palmer up and dropped him on his bed. Kind of him, Palmer managed to think through the pain and blurred vision before passing out.

When he came to, his hand went to where he kept his purse. It was gone.

He cursed. When he tried to sit up, the pain in his body forbade it. Instead he had to roll over and up until he was seated on the end of his bed. He was able to stand, just. He was not able to lift his door back into position. Well, there was little or nothing left in the room worth stealing.

The worst of the discomfort would come tomorrow, he knew. Meantime, he had to get his door fixed and for that he needed money. He would have to pay a call on the goldsmith at Cheapside for funds to replace what he had lost. He carefully avoided limping past Wilkins's tavern.

The money got and a workman despatched to make the necessary repair, Palmer made his way back to the Bell. Alcohol would ease the pain in the short term.

The landlord saw that Palmer had been in the wars. He knew better than to ask why.

'Wilkins,' was all Palmer would say, easing himself painfully onto a stool.

'Nasty piece o' work,' the landlord said.

And the meek shall inherit the earth? Palmer tried not to laugh.

~ 17 ~

THE HOUSE in the former monastery of Blackfriars was not what might be expected for a woman who liked to style herself fourth in line to the Throne.

Two guests, both women, were introduced into it by the porter. An older woman greeted them more formally inside.

'My Lady Cumberland,' the woman said, smiling.

'Mrs Talbot.'

'This is your waiting woman?' Mrs Talbot asked, who filled that role herself for her niece, the lady of the house.

'And my *friend*, Mrs Lanier, Emilia Lanier.'

'My husband is...'

'We talk of no husbands here,' Mrs Talbot cut Emilia off . 'My Lady Arbella is waiting for you in the library.'

Lady Arbella Stuart was a notorious bookworm, that much everyone knew so the two women were not surprised to find her seated and reading, a tiny dog on her lap. With a start, Emilia recognised the book, of sonnets, by the actor she had once known and used, and been used by, to her annoyance. Did the Lady know? She showed no sign.

Lady Arbella had the plump face of a child's turning to middle-aged jowls. Rouge attempted to disguise a recent attack of smallpox she was lucky to have survived. She remained seated, extending her hand to be kissed by both women. Lady Cumberland made the introductions.

'Are you proud, Mrs Lanier?' Lady Arbella asked out of nowhere.

Emilia nearly blushed under her olive skin.

'They say I am proud,' Lady Arbella went on without waiting for an answer. 'But then, my great-grandfather was Henry Tudor, King of England, the Seventh of that name.'

Emilia gave an inclination of her head in recognition.

'My claim to the Throne is as good as my cousin James's, with one omission...'

Everyone knew what it was.

'... that I am a woman.'

There was no answer the visitors could, or should give. Talk of royal succession was deemed treasonous in private as well as in public.

'And so here I sit, at four and thirty, dependant on dole from my *generous* cousin His Majesty, with no husband, no children and no household to talk of, beyond my beloved Aunt Mary.'

She threw a loving glance to Mrs Talbot who returned it.

'He will not let me marry, you see.'

Everyone knew the story, the projected marriages which had never happened, to a Dudley, to a Catholic Farnese; most scandalously of all and not so long past, a failed elopement with a Seymour, that tainted family with risky royal blood in their veins. Plotters had twice attempted to hoist her, willing or unwilling onto the Throne in the Catholic interest. She was seen by some as the Mary, Queen of Scots of the day, a double-edged recognition.

'I write letters, letter after letter, of begging, of complaint...'

They were no longer read by the men in charge.

'... but I *shall* surprise them, yes I shall, soon, soon.'

The look she gave Lady Cumberland and Emilia Lanier was a mixture of desperation and flirtatiousness. Then it changed to something more businesslike.

'Now, Mrs Lanier, let us talk of the *book* you wish to dedicate to me.'

'Mr Shakespeare introduces the masque into his work, thankfully not a long one.'

The odd character muttering to himself was a known criticaster, or critic.

Onstage below him in the draughty old Banqueting House in Whitehall, around the sleeping hero of the *Cymbeline* play, four ghosts in white robes moved in measured procession to the music of the grave making a joint invocation to the powers above.

Thunder sheets flexed and roared, lightning appeared to shoot from the heavens.

'Ingenious, our Mr Inigo,' the critic said to no-one in particular.

Descending from on high on a gold-gilt chair modelled to resemble an eagle, Jupiter, chief of the gods gestured with angry, pointing finger at the earthlings cowering below. Another clap of thunder struck, a flare onstage lit up to create the effect of a thunderbolt landing.

No more, you petty spirits of region low, offend our hearing!

Jupiter's robe of imperial purple caught the light and uplit the god's face, his beard curling magnificently. The actor underneath it was Henry Condell standing in for John Hemmings.

'I'm not going anywhere on *that*!' the older actor had protested at the sight of Inigo Jones's machine, an apparatus new to the King's Men.

Hemmings was determined to keep his feet firmly on the stage. There was to be no cranking down from the ceiling for him.

Condell had no such fears. As great Jupiter, he gave his final command.

Mount, Eagle, to my palace crystalline.

The critic tittered. It was...

'... too much, too much!'

After an initial jolt the eagle and its god swept smoothly back into the heavens. Applause broke out for the stage deity and for another, more important god sitting among them – the benevolent King James who acknowledged the tribute with a wave of his royal hand. Near him, not so near as to offend Queen Anne in public, sat the King's new favourite, Robbie Carr, pink and ginger in the Scottish taste.

'No wonder they now live apart,' the critic said, looking at the royal couple.

He went ignored by those around him who could not afford to hear such things.

Cymbeline was a long, long evening.

Relieved of Revels duties, Palmer spent the midwinter festival in Oxford with the Davenants.

'She never speaks about her mother,' Jane Davenant said. 'We treat her as one of our own.'

Together they were watching the little girl, lips pursed, eyes serious, spinning the top which Palmer had brought with him for her. How it gyrated forever, she didn't ask, to Palmer's relief who could not have explained it. She was not yet at the age of 'why?'

When Miracle was in bed and John Davenant had time to join his wife, Palmer told them more about Ellen's fate and where she was buried. He did not fail to name Wilkins.

'The man should be taken before the Justices. He should be hanged – and all the rest of it!'

Both men swapped glances at the passionate words of the woman between them.

'I fear there is little the Law can do,' John Davenant said.

'Then God curse him!' said his wife.

'And what will you do now, Richard?' Davenant asked Palmer.

It was difficult for Palmer to answer. What did a man do at his time of life? What new directions could he take? There were plenty he knew had not made it to his age, closer to fifty than forty.

'Something will turn up,' he said.

'God willing,' Davenant added.

Clapping Palmer on the shoulder, he signalled for another pot of beer.

~ 18 ~

THE COLD WINTER gave way to the promise of spring but with no let up from the plague. Plans to reopen the Globe for its regular summer season were set back once again.

'Seventy pounds,' John Hemmings reported.

It was the compensation he had received from the royal purse on behalf of the King's Men for their unemployment during the continuing pestilence.

'Better than we'd have got under the old Queen.'

The men were pleased that Hemmings had achieved something to help keep bodies and souls together. It was worth pounds each for the sharers and useful shillings for the hired men but it was nothing like what they could earn with the Globe open and it did nothing to advance any plans they had for the Blackfriars playhouse. Was the second year of their taking it back to pass with nothing staged there, nothing achieved?

'Tilney's not looking good,' Hemmings added, about the Master of the Revels through whom the compensation had been settled. 'On his last legs if you ask me.'

Already there was talk of shifting the Revels office from Clerkenwell to St Peter's Hill, near St Paul's 'when the time came', when Tilney left the scene.

'How long has Tilney been at it?' Cuthbert Burbage asked.

Hemmings answered the question.

'Since before my time. He goes back to your father's time, Cuthbert, when the first theatres were built, back in the seventies, more than thirty years ago.'

167

This was longer than some men lived, poor Ned Shakespeare for a start.

All of a sudden, reported cases of the plague dwindled. Government relaxed its prohibition on public gatherings and entertainments.

Now it was all hands on board as the Globe prepared to reopen. The banging and knocking of carpenters and joiners, repairing and making good or making new, punctuated the other business of the place – the cleaning and the fitting out, and the chatter of those brought in to tally at the doors and the calls of the girls selling the nuts and fruit and ale, feeding the workers. Out went men to post playbills in public places to spread the word, that the Globe and all its wonders were once again open for the pleasure of London audiences and its visitors.

While the world waited for the opening day, the tiring house people busied themselves with the wardrobe and the arms and armour, the small ordnance and all the properties needed to mount a successful season of plays. The bookman worked on copying out playrolls needed by the actors, one for each in each play. Some were new to their parts, given their opportunities by the effects of death and disease on the company which was back to full strength, in the mid-twenties in number.

'What have we got, Will?'

Cuthbert Burbage was the asker, the man of business for the playhouse as opposed to the company's who was Hemmings.

'We have *Cymbeline*, that's new to the London public.'

'And what shall we revive?'

'I talked to your brother Richard...'

The leading man and the main draw for a public deprived of him for over a season.

'... and the play he wants is – *Othello*.'

It was one of Dick's big parts and the public liked it, titillated by a black man and a white woman mixed up in sexual jealousy and intrigue. The play had done well four years ago.

'Dick loves blacking up!'

Put out the light...

The flame of the candle was hardly visible in the late afternoon light on this last day of April. A trace of smoke betrayed that it had been lit and was now extinguished.

... and then put out the light.

The meaning was clear. Striding towards the recess at the back of the stage, a black figure drew back the curtains to show his young wife in her white wedding night shift sleeping in the marital bed. He flexed his outstretched hands for all the crowd to see, black as his exposed body. An excited gasp betrayed what they expected to see next.

Palmer, stuck in among the stink of the groundlings in front of the stage, was straining to see. There was no business in the Globe for him. He had drifted there for something to do which, at the cost of a penny, was cheaper than passing his time

in the Bell Inn. It was unlike him to feel the need to be among
people.

The crowd fell silent, even the groundlings around him as
the play ground to its inevitable conclusion over the strangled
body of the unfortunate wife. It needed the out-of-place song
and dance reinstated at the end of the show to get them back
into their holiday mood.

On his way out of the playhouse, a woman's voice halted
him. Sight of her face confirmed his suspicion – it was Emilia
Lanier, standing next to a dubious-looking character.

She introduced him.

'Mr Simon Forman, my doctor and astrologer.'

Palmer knew the name. He had once followed the
Alderman's wife to Forman's lodgings. He knew his reputation,
for taking his fees in kind especially where his clients were
anxious about their fertility. Forman was notorious for it.

'What do you take the moral of the play to be, Mr
Palmer?' the quack asked.

'Keep a close eye on your pocket linen.'

Forman did not laugh.

They walked all three together to the river's edge. Forman
offered to share a boat going upstream but Emilia appeared to
want to talk to Palmer on her own.

'My Ladies Cumberland and Dorset are in town,' she
announced, offering Palmer a place in her boat.

Out into the mainstream of the river, she spoke what was
really on her mind.

'I understand you know the world of books, the publishers
and printers. I have a work which merits setting before the
public.'

Oh yes, and what might it be, Palmer wondered? An awful
thought crossed his mind, that Lady Cumberland wanted her
pieties put into print. He had heard of noble ladies putting pen

to parchment for circulation among their own sort, but going into print, exposing one's ladylike self to the public eye, that was unheard of!

He remembered what her husband had told him, about Emilia's ambitions. So far she had not asked him, as her husband had, for her sonnets back.

'Who is the author?' Palmer dutifully asked. 'What is the subject?'

Lanier *had* said. The author was Emilia.

'I call it *Salve Deus Rex Judaeorum*. The title came to me in a dream – All Hail O God and King of the Jews!'

'Yes, I know what it means, what is it about?'

'I describe the passion of Our Lord and of the women who followed him, returning us to our honoured place of womanly virtue. I sing the merits of my Lady Cumberland...'

She stopped, seeing the interest go out of her listener's eyes.

'... there is also a pastoral poem on the estate at Cookham where I was privileged to serve her.'

It appeared to make no difference to Palmer.

'I believe I can secure the patronage of important ladies in my lady's circle – Lady Pembroke for example, and others of her character...'

The Pembroke name counted, Palmer conceded with a grunt. The Pembroke sons were high at Court, destined, it was said, for prominent public office. King James liked the look of them, which was recommendation enough. The old Countess herself was a Sidney, a powerful family with writers among them, her included.

'... Lady Bedford, Lady Suffolk ... my Lady Dorset of course – beloved Anne – and my old patroness Lady Kent...'

Ah yes, Kent, where they had both come in together all those years ago, when Emilia had left him behind in favour of London and all its conceits.

It was all such a long time ago, Palmer told himself, when his father was still busying himself in religious protest, protest leading to persecution by the State, punishment coming in the form of heavier and heavier fines and the loss of everything generations of Palmers had built up over centuries. Palmer the reluctant investigator, placeless, and the family's best bed was the sum total of the Palmer inheritance surviving.

Maybe Emilia had been prescient about his future prospects, back in the days of Kent?

'.... and the patronage of His Majesty's cousin, the Lady Arbella Stuart,' he heard her add to her list of notables.

She had kept her strongest card till last, or so she reckoned from the look Palmer saw on her face.

'Why not the Queen?' Palmer asked.

Emilia ignored the joke.

'Perhaps I *shall* invite her, wronged woman as she also is.'

This was dangerous talk. Seeming to sense it, Emilia moderated herself.

'You have heard about the latest masque intended for the Court?'

Palmer allowed her to enlighten him.

'*Oberon*, by Messers Jonson and Jones. Prince Henry is to dance in it. My cousin Robert Johnson is writing the music together with my nephew Ferrabosco – nephew by marriage but family all the same. I am to be there, I may have the opportunity to be presented to Her Majesty. If I am...'

Always ambitious, Palmer thought, seeing the unstoppable woman in front of him, never one to be kept down. He gave her a fresh look. She was no longer using art to cover the grey which flecked the mane of dark hair she had always been so proud of, brushed back from a forehead more lined than smooth these days. Her olive skin was tauter and shinier than its softness in her youth. She was careful not to show her teeth – her once frequent laughter absented itself.

Ferrabosco, she'd said?

Was this the same Ferrabosco who had written the music for Jonson's arse-numbing masque he'd once endured, the one about marriage? Ferraboscos, Bassanos, Laniers, like a musical round in and out of each other's beds generation after generation, legally and not and now with Emilia's own son, Henry, busy joining them in the same dance.

'Are you looking to make money out of this?' Palmer asked Emilia.

A look of offence at his question gave him his answer.

A thought detained Palmer. The work *was* religious – religion sold well in difficult times, plague times like the present. Richard Field the publisher had told him as much years ago when he had first pursued the man Shakespeare. And Emilia had noble names to stir into the pot. He had never thought of a woman in print, it was a novelty, and novelty, he had learned, sold.

'My advice is...'

'Have you seen *Shakespeare's Sonnets*?' Emilia asked, cutting him off.

Seen them? He was the cause of their publication. He limited himself to saying that he had.

'I believe they deserve answering,' Emilia said. 'Our mother Eve was deceived by such cunning.'

'By the Serpent,' Palmer said.

'But surely Adam cannot be excused, he was most to blame.'

'If I were to find you a publisher,' Palmer started to say, moving the subject on, 'a reputable publisher, your fee would not be large.'

Not for such a strange work, for a work by a woman however novel it was.

'You can keep a tithe of the fee yourself,' Emilia said.

A tenth part? Shillings, all the same worth several weeks of drinking at the Bell.

'I shall need to see the text.'

'Where shall I send it?'

To the landlord at the Bell Inn, Carter Lane, Palmer told her. It was his reading room.

A day later, he settled down to it with his customary pot of ale.

Words in front of him rolled by in steady ten-beat verse. Emilia was plainly making up to her mistress Lady C, penning her lessons of Christian endurance.

> *Thy patience, faith, long suffering, and thy love*
> *He will reward with comforts from above.*

What was it with poets, Palmer asked himself, sipping more beer, always trying to teach their betters? The sonnets in his chamber started in just the same way, claiming an easy intimacy between the praiser and the praised.

Ancient shades of his favourite Roman poets reproached him. Patrons were fair game. A game it had always had been.

As he put the pot down, Emilia's verse turned to warning.

But woe to them that double-hearted be,
Who with their tongues the righteous souls do slay.

It was a warning to those who...

... let their arrows flee
To wound true hearted people anyway...
Deceitful tongues are but false slander's wings.

Could certain sonnets be guilty of her charge, the ones written by Shakespeare? The Lord would smite them, Palmer smiled as he read. There was plenty of brimstone here to please the prejudices of Emilia's moral ladies. Renunciation too.

That outward beauty which the world commends,
Is not the subject I will write upon.

No, not now that her own glory days were past.

A mind enriched with virtue shines more bright.

Beauty had ensnared so many, the poetry complained – Helen of Troy, chaste Lucrece and the wronged wife of Mark Anthony, husband-loser to Cleopatra.

Hadn't Shakespeare handled them too, Palmer quarrelled with her mentally? And what about you in the bed of the powerful lord you betrayed with a poet and his muse? You could have stayed in Kent and found a respectable husband. Are you really the falsely seduced maiden? Is that how you tell the story to your circle of moral ladies? Is it how they like to hear it, priapic desire responsible for all the world's ills?

It takes two to tangle, Palmer told himself firmly.

Emilia was away, into Jesus, his death and suffering.

But my dear muse, now whither would'st thou fly,
Above the pitch of thy appointed strain?

Right!

But thy poor infant verse must soar aloft....

There was no stopping her or any poet, Palmer reflected. This poet and the other one shared more in common than they knew.

He followed her in Christ's shoes into the garden of Gethsemane. The wife of Pontius Pilate spoke up for Christ and for all women. Man stood accused. Eve obeyed the Serpent? Men killed Christ. Men came into the world through women's pain. Christ mounted Calvary with women's qualities – *virtue, patience, grace, love, piety* – claims not lost even on the reader in Carter Lane.

Hail Mary full of grace gave no shock to the Catholic-born Palmer or the stanzas of Mariolatry which followed. She wrote the Passion well, he thought, as well as any devotee now or before. Her description of the beauty of the dead Christ created images in Palmer's mind of altarpieces seen in Catholic lands on campaign, a legacy of her Italian blood?

She was free with classical allusion too. Cleopatra stood compared to her lady patroness.

... yet thou a black Egyptian dost appear,
Thou false, she true.

Black had been bandied about in the other poet's sonnets to his false mistress. Was there irony in Emilia's words, Palmer wondered?

'You back in the Revels business?' the landlord interrupted him from over his shoulder.

Palmer shrugged.

'What's this 'un about?' the landlord asked, looking down at the manuscript Palmer was reading.

'Woman's work,' Palmer said.

'Woman's work?'

The landlord went on his way.

Palmer put the script down. There was only one way to find out the value of what he had in front of him. He must try it out on the publishing trade.

His first port of call was with Richard Field in Blackfriars. Palmer had not seen him since the trouble caused by the Earl of Essex when Field had been a publisher of religious works as well as those of his boyhood friend from Stratford, William Shakespeare.

The man was no less dapper than before, Palmer could see. Then so many futures including Field's own had been thrown into the balance by an ill-advised play performed to get the mob in the mood for regicide. Yes, Field had heard the cock crow mightily loudly at the time, shifting any blame onto his writer friend.

'What I am looking for is advice,' Palmer craftily asked.

Field asked for time to read the work. He set a time for Palmer to return two days hence.

'It's not for us,' was his verdict when they met again.

It never had been. The last thing in the world he intended to do was to have dealings with a man who had once caused him so much worry and trouble.

'What is your judgement about the quality of it?' Palmer asked him. 'What about its argument?'

Field stroked his natty beard, cut narrow in the latest style.

'If there was a market for women buying books......'

'She has plenty of fine patrons, the sort of women who have libraries.'

'A handful of sales. It's not for us.'

'Who might it be for?'

Field was unforthcoming.

'Blount?' Palmer suggested.

'You could try Blount,' Field said.

Yes, Palmer could try Blount. The answer would be the same. Let him try Blount. It was a good enough way of getting rid of the man.

Blount's verdict was no different but he gave the matter closer thought.

'There's no doubt that a woman writer's an unusual thing,' he said, 'and her argument doesn't lack spirit. All the same, it would be a bold man who would publish it.'

'Why? Because it is...'

Palmer searched for the word, one he had heard Buc use.

'... controversial?'

'No, no,' Blount laughed, 'pounds, shillings and pence bold. I doubt if a publisher would get his money back.'

Palmer put down his last card. He told Blount something of Emilia's colourful past as the mistress of the old Lord Chamberlain, hinting at her role in the triangle in the sonnets.

'So, she has a story behind her,' Blount said. 'I *have* heard that Lord Southampton was not best pleased by the publication. It would be a bold man – a rash one some might say – who would risk banging this partic'lar drum to annoy the ears of such a powerful man.'

Palmer's eyes pressed him.

'There is Gosson of course, he likes a fight.'

Where had he heard that name, Palmer asked himself? Publisher of George Wilkins. No!

'There's one other. Have you heard of...

Richard Bonian. At least he did not look the dubious sort when Palmer met him.

'I hear you published *Troilus & Cressida* last year,' he said, using the information Blount had given him about the fate of Shakespeare's Trojan play.

'Have you read it?'

Palmer had, in the Revels office, and said so.

'It is interesting for the stance it takes – Achilles and all the rest of the heroes in their worst human colours.'

Bonian looked again at the man in front of him. Palmer's reputation had preceded him. All the same, an informer might have something useful for a printer on the lookout for what sells.

'What if I suggest,' Palmer started to say, 'that this particular Cressida has, in this work of hers, something to say for herself, in her own words?'

Palmer repeated what he had told Blount about Emilia.

'You are saying she is the dark woman of the sonnets?'

'Is that what they are calling her?'

'There has been much speculation,' Bonian said, 'all sorts of fine ladies fingered, but I must say, Mistress Lanier makes good sense.'

Bonian leaned forward.

'Leave the manuscript with me and come back in an hour. If she can write, can write at all, I think there is a market for her.'

'You have no concerns about her reputation? Or the hostility of Lord Southampton?'

'The opposite, Mr Palmer, the opposite. If she presents herself, as you say, as a woman reformed, who could say anything against this Magdalene?'

~ 19 ~

THE FEE Bonian offered was reduced from the standard five pounds to four, handsome enough money as far as Palmer was concerned given the eight silver shillings he set aside for himself. Four of them bore the sharp-faced profile of the old Queen, living on in her sound currency.

'We have too much on for the time being,' Bonian told him, 'so I shan't register it until the autumn. Tell Mrs Lanier she can expect publication next year. Meantime, no tricks, Mr Palmer, we have an agreement and you have my money.'

Palmer was not offended. The man's concern for his new property reassured him. It meant he saw something in it. He took the news and the money back to Emilia.

She was pleased.

'I shall want copies for my friends,' she said, meaning her great ladies, Lady Cumberland and her circle. And why not the Queen? And her royal son and daughter? And...

'I have already made the deal,' Palmer said.

The pair looked at each other.

'So what now for you, Mr Palmer?' Emilia asked. 'Back to your old employment?'

So she knew about his exit from the Revels office.

'And you?' Palmer countered. 'Authorship pays only so much. Is Master Lanier in funds?'

Palmer doubted if he was.

'I find my own way,' Emilia said, anger rising in her face. 'I shall not want your services again.'

The eight shillings came in handy to Palmer.

It would have been just as welcome to any of the King's Men.

'I cannot believe it!' Hemmings protested at the news that, once again, the playhouses were to be closed due to a fresh surge in plague cases. 'It's as bad as the early nineties, and they nearly finished us off!'

The great plague of that time was legend in the actors' world. It had brought about a revolution among the acting companies, some amalgamating, some dying on their feet as the new wave killed off the old. Hemmings had no desire to be washed up and out of work, not at his time of life. He was too old to go back to his old grocer's trade.

How could the actors fight back?

There was no choice but to try more of the same, a remedy agreed by Cuthbert Burbage – more touring, more sales to publishers of unneeded plays and hopes for a good Court season come the winter. At least James was more generous than Elizabeth had ever been.

'Oxford will take us in September,' Hemmings said, 'and we have Jonson's latest play for them, his *Alchemist* – that will please them.'

'We *must* do something with the Blackfriars,' Cuthbert Burbage reminded everyone.

As the man responsible for the company's two playhouses, he understood best how they were money-pits if they weren't put to work.

'… so let's hope for Easter next year.'

As late as that? Hemmings groaned. Two years lost, near as.

Flush with cash, Palmer decided on a spree away from the Bell Inn.

He chose the Mermaid Tavern, last visited when he was in pursuit of Ben Jonson in Gunpowder time. It came as a surprise to him, and then on reflection not to find the selfsame man there, an even bigger slab of lard than he was before, including at their altercation during *Romeo & Juliet*.

Jonson was deep in conversation with the landlord. Some things did not change, Palmer was satisfied to see. He made his way to a quiet corner, content to drink and watch the world go by. It remained to be seen whether a quiet drink would turn into several noisy ones.

'I thought it was you, Palmer. Or should I say, Mr W.H.?'

Palmer heard Jonson's once-familiar voice over him. Jonson let out a hearty belch as he swung his ham of a leg over a stool opposite.

'Is it true? I must say, I've been telling everyone it is. *What* a joke! Poor old Will, caught by the coillons and exposed to public view as a love-sick swain!'

Palmer did not answer the question. He asked instead what Jonson was up to and was promptly told all about it.

'I expect an *enormous* success with my *Alchemist* – the clue's in the title, all very Dr Dee – once it is staged. It was marked down for the Globe until plague shut it down. Still, Oxford calls, and after that the Court.'

Oxford, Palmer thought, and of the Davenants and little Miracle. He swept aside an irritating stab of sentiment.

Jonson ran on in full spate.

'I have a great deal of fun keeping the play true to the Unities, of time and place and so on. It should please the old stick-in-the-muds on that count alone.'

One of those himself, Palmer listened with a flickering of respect.

'Next up I shall return to the classics and the higher learning – fully earned, I may say, after the swill I am called on to throw to the groundlings in the public playhouse. I have a mind to do the Catiline conspiracy. Mean anything to you, Palmer?'

'The Roman Republic saved, Cicero the prosecutor...'

Jonson was momentarily surprised.

'Just so, just so. There is scope for great speeches...'

Palmer yawned – they wouldn't be short, not once Jonson had wrung every last inch of long-wordery out of it.

'... and we know about interrogation, some of us.'

Jonson had been scorched in the Gunpowder plot. A shared religion with the men behind it and dinners with them in private had very nearly brought him down, his poetic wings melted in the fire of Government fury. Palmer had witnessed his fall and his surprising resurrection.

'Shall we be seeing more of you here?' Jonson asked.

It was not a friendly request.

'... you see, the landlord is planning to bring back my club of bantering wits here at the Mermaid but you will understand it if I say that it is not something someone of your kind would enjoy. And my friends would *smell* you.'

Palmer smiled palely, enough to show that he was not about to move until he was ready to.

Jonson was not finished with him.

'Sir George Buc, now ... now that Tilney's dead...'

'Dead?'

It was the first Palmer had heard of it.

'Yes, dead, made his will, took to his bed, extinct a month after. *Sic transit.*'

Poor old Tilney, Palmer thought, but old he was, well over the biblical three score and ten. Would Jonson make such a score? Would he, Palmer? Did he want to?

'My question is this, about Buc. Is he a man of a *strong* constitution?'

Palmer divined what was behind the question – Jonson had ambitions to be Master of the Revels in succession to Buc … more like the Lord of Misrule, he couldn't help thinking, looking at the mini-man-mountain in front of him. Well, disease might take anyone at any time so there was no merit in prediction unless you were the Forman astrologer type. But if life took its normal course, he would bet on the slab in front of him going first. Buc was the lean and hungry sort after all.

'The price of reversions goes up every day,' he said.

'I have friends, Palmer,' Jonson said, hauling his bulk up from the stool, 'I have friends.'

For the first time in a long time, Palmer walked past Wilkins's tavern. It was quieter than usual.

A figure slid out of the door ahead of him, Thomas Thorpe the publisher. Thorpe saw him too but not quickly enough to avoid being taken forcibly by the arm and walked away along the street.

'I'm surprised to find you in such a low establishment,' Palmer whispered in his ear.

'Business, Mr Palmer, business.'

'Has Wilkins been busy with the pen?'

'With the law courts, with the law courts.'

Palmer was all ears.

'Assault on a man and his doxy,' Thorpe said.

Well there was a surprise!

'And don't tell me, you stood bail for him.'

'No ... no, no. Gosson did that.'

Publisher of the *Pericles* romance – as Palmer had seen in the Revels office.

'So what was this business?'

'A matter of conscience, yes, conscience.'

Palmer smelled religion. He knew about Thorpe's proclivities carried as far as Madrid, but Wilkins too? It all helped build the case against the man. He had not forgotten Ellen.

'And how are the *Sonnets* selling?' Palmer asked.

'Ah yes ... selling ... they are selling ... they are sold.'

Another visit from one of Lord Southampton's men had finally put paid to their progress through Elde's printing press, along with the information that his lordship had spoken a few choice words into the ear of the Bishop of London, for his censor-man's benefit. Thorpe was not going to be allowed to make his fortune from them.

Now he faced Palmer.

With a pleading squint of his eyes, he scuttled away down a convenient sidestreet.

Palmer's discovery, that the Chief Minister's old official had a taste for sack , the strong wine of Spain, rather than beer made their next meeting more revealing.

'The great contract is failing,' the Whitehall man confessed to Palmer after his third cup. 'The King is adamant that a definite annual income must be followed by a lump sum to pay off his accumulated debts. Of course, Parliament wants the first but not the second.'

'What else is concerning Lord Salisbury?' Palmer asked.

'Now that Prince Henry has been installed as Prince of Wales...'

The ageing man's eyes glowed at the memory of the Prince's ceremony. It had been a dazzling affair in the midst of the Commons and Lords in Westminster. King Arthur and his Round Table could not have done better!

His hand reached for his cup of wine so that he could silently toast himself for the days he had spent burrowing into ancient sources, compiling work his master was pleased to claim credit for himself, as was only meet and proper.

'... he is making his voice heard. His Royal Highness is strong in the faith...'

Meaning the new one, Palmer understood, not the old.

'... so he will not, *will not*, marry a Catholic princess. This disappoints His Majesty and the Chief Minister too. The requirement of State is for closer alliance with Spain or with France – Catholic kingdoms both – especially after the dreadful business last May...'

The assassination of King Henri of France, a Protestant who had thought Paris worth a mass and conversion to Rome a fair price to pay for a throne. No breastplate against an assassin's dagger, however.

'... yes, quite dreadful. It counsels my master to remain as flexible as possible in the matter of a royal marriage for our fine Prince and future King.'

'Speaking of Catholics...' Palmer started to say, determined to introduce what he had learned about Thorpe and Wilkins and why the tavern-keeper merited punishment.

The official heard him out.

'Wilkins is hardly worth bothering about,' he replied. 'The Chief Minister has the awkward business of the Lady Arbella on our hands – much more important.'

Palmer's ears perked up – Lady Arbella Stuart was the King's first cousin and, on and off, next in line to the Throne after the royal family. More to the point, she was one of Emilia's circle, or was likely to be if Emilia had her way with the smooth words of dedication she was planning at the front of her book. Emilia, Palmer had reason to know, never believed in starting low.

'Whitehall is buzzing with Lady Arbella's latest escapade,' the official said.

It was a secret marriage.

A wise lady but unstable, was the view Palmer now heard from the official, about a woman past thirty-five and desperate to be married. But marriage risked children, and King James had no desire to see rival claimants to the Throne. It didn't help that the Lady Arbella had been touted early in the reign as a convenient replacement for the Scottish King – even the Pope in Rome had made her case. She was an intolerable risk, a threat to the established order was the party line which Palmer now heard.

'She has these quite fantastic delusions about her prospects,' the old official said, loyal to the Stuart as he had been to the Tudor line despite both sweeping his own religion aside. He had read her many letters of complaint.

'Is it true she's married young Seymour?' Palmer asked.

The older brother had been the cause of a similar scandal with the lady some years before.

He knew the answer to his question. Why else was the lad, a dozen years her junior, locked up in the Tower himself? The Seymours had too many royal ancestors of their own for safety in an age when descent from a chamber servant who had got his leg over a royal widow had been title enough for the Tudors to gain the Throne.

'Yes, it is true, despite the strongest of warnings from His Majesty. She's been sent to a trusted guardian in Lambeth.'

'And had the knot been cut?'

'You are indelicate, Mr Palmer,' the old official giggled, looking at his empty cup.

Palmer called for another, one ear on the official's answer.

'... but that's the fear, right enough. Somehow she got herself into the Tower with Seymour and the word is,' the man giggled again, 'she may be with child. But about – what was his name, Wilkins?' he said. 'Work with the Law, Mr Palmer, work with the Law.'

'What do you mean by that?'

'A murderer may escape the highest penalty, but if he does not pay his taxes...'

'Wilkins does not pay his taxes?'

'A hypothesis, Mr Palmer, a hypothethesis. You say the man is a licensed victualler. Is he fit to hold that license?'

Palmer began to see. Wilkins had been up in front of the Justices often enough. He locked the thought away.

'About the Lady Arbella, if the Chief Minister is in need of any help...' he started to say, anxious to gain something positive from the meeting, something money-making.

'I had wondered about that myself, indeed, I had a word with the Chief Minister about it. The King is outraged by her marrying without his permission which is required under the Law.'

He was outraged by more than that, both men understood.

'Unfortunately, Lady Arbella now requires restraint,' the old official said, 'and from her own foolishness, restraint *sine die* or so I fear. So I do not see how you can help us there.'

A few weeks later, Lady Arbella's story took another playhouse turn. Palmer heard the truth of it from the same source.

'She was arrested on the high seas. She was being posted north to Durham but escaped on the road in Barnet. She made her way, disguised as a boy...'

Disguised as a boy? Palmer heard the quills of a dozen hack playwrights sharpening at the report.

'... to Blackwall where she planned to meet up with her Seymour swain only he ducked out and made an alternative exit abroad. Her ship to the Netherlands was overtaken.'

It was a story as far-fetched as anything Palmer had been forced to watch at the Globe including the perennial girl-dressed-as-boy. Whatever he had wished for, he was relieved he had not got the case with the sad lady now back stifling in the Tower. He was no gaoler – the one time when he had tried to be he had very nearly lost his man. But he was still in need of work. This latest evening of beer and sack with the old official was so far only seeing his savings dwindle.

The old official did not dwell on the royal lady.

'My lord the Chief Minister is not well,' he said, swirling his own future round the cup in front of him. 'I fear it is the lungs.'

Palmer had heard it was the pox caught from his respectable mistress who'd had it from her not-so-respectable husband, one of Salisbury's fellow Privy Councillors and another play-loving potentate.

'... he is as thin as a rake, he coughs excessively. His sputum is flecked with blood – I have seen it, yes, I have seen it. Yet he will not let up on his work.'

The illness was bad news for both men drinking together.

'It is a shame we never could persuade Mr Shakespeare to let us use the *Timon* play,' the Whitehall man lamented. 'A parable is worth a thousand good arguments when it comes to persuading princes of their obligations. Was it ever performed?'

'Not to my knowledge,' Palmer said, looking glumly into his beer.

'Do you think...?'

The old official was beginning to speculate but Palmer cut him off.

'Not Shakespeare, no, he's made his mind up not to finish it.'

But what ... what if if Shakespeare was not involved in the decision, Palmer asked himself?

He called for more drinks.

~ 20 ~

'IT IS *SHOCKING*, this treatment of Lady Arbella.'

Emilia Lanier spoke passionately – her ladyship was of Stuart royal blood so why hadn't they treated her as such, why were they not treating her better? It was so frustrating, most of all for the hopes Emilia had placed on the royal lady patronising her book.

What could be done to retrieve the situation?

She apologised for speaking so boldly among her betters in the prayer group led by Lady Cumberland. It was a rare outing for Emilia, one of the few acceptable pretexts for the two classes of women to meet now that Cookham was behind them. Both were remembering the last interview with the ill-starred lady in her library in Blackfriars.

'You speak justly in the eyes of God,' her patroness said. 'If we could help her, we would, but what is it we can do? We must pray for her.'

'Yes,' Emilia said, 'let us pray for her,' barely hiding her disappointment.

Prayer did not prevent her from feeling badly let down. Why was she blocked at every turn? Her golden days with Hunsdon, crushed by unwanted pregnancy, her husband a failure, worse, cruel and rapacious, her one child set to enjoy no higher status than the rest of her unremarked family, the other children she had lost. Redemption at the hands of Lady Cumberland had been reduced by the lady's own husband troubles. In every case, her knockbacks were the work of men.

And yet, and yet – the gorgeous clothes and the glinting jewels of her glory days, fine dancing to the best musicians, her kin watching her take her place among the high and mighty in soft candlelight throwing shadows of the beautiful and the powerful onto myth-laden tapestries; unending tables of food, wines rich as ruby and gold and above all, eyes, men's eyes, fixed in lust, on her.

She sighed, turning her mind to more practical things. Bonian had at last registered his intention to publish *Salve Deus.* Her energies must be invested in the use she would make of the book due to be published in the coming year.

'I *shall* surprise them.'

Lady Arbella's words came back to Emilia. So she would too.

Palmer was running short of money. It kept him home more than he wanted and away from Christmas in Oxford with the Davenants.

The Chief Minister's official treated him to a night at the Bell Inn. The Christmas festivities were in full swing at the Court, Palmer was bored to hear because he was made to listen to tales of Jonson acting cock of the walk and the King's Men busily employed. Everyone except himself was being well rewarded, it was a merry Christmas for everyone but him.

'In the masque, our young Hyperion, the Prince of Wales led out his mother in the dance. Little Princess Elizabeth followed, led out by Lord Southampton.'

The Whitehall man did not see the effect of what he was saying. Palmer laughed, a bitter sound. He had once saved the Princess from capture by unscrupulous, faith-crazed men. He had seen Southampton where he had deserved to be, in the Tower.

The official asked what was so funny. Palmer told him.

'Next you'll be telling me George Wilkins has a pension from the King!'

It was enough to turn Palmer's thoughts back to the *Timon* play.

He bided his time until he was rewarded by the news he wanted – William Shakespeare had gone away to spend the winter in Stratford. Palmer made his way to the Blackfriars playhouse where he knew he would find the King's Men rehearsing the plays they were putting on at Court.

'What do you want, Palmer?'

The challenge from John Hemmings was markedly unfriendly as Palmer knew it would be, now that he was out of office.

'I have a proposal,' Palmer said.

It was about a private reading of an out-of-date play. It was about *Timon*.

Hemmings bristled. Both men knew how much trouble a special show had caused a decade before when the actors put one on intended – not that they knew it – to excite the mob to revolution. The name of the play, *Richard II*, went unspoken by many to this day. Only recently had it been permitted to republish it in full.

'This is different,' Palmer said before Hemmings had time to cut him short. 'The Chief Minister has always wanted to hear *Timon*.'

'Oh that one! It was never finished. Will – Mr Shakespeare – would never approve...'

'But he's not here, is he? And the play is not entirely his. Wouldn't Mr Middleton value the opportunity for *his* hand in the work to be heard? I'm not proposing a public performance, not like the Richard play. It will be entirely private.'

'Why?'

Hemmings's question was blunt.

'The Chief Minister is not well.'

Hemmings raised an eyebrow. He had heard rumours, he had seen the man close to at Court. It figured.

'And so?' he asked.

'Wouldn't you humour a dying man who can get the Privy Council to open the playhouses again, who can face down the disapprovers who will use the plague reports against you for as a long as there is a single case over the odds reported?'

Hemmings gave Palmer a long, hard look.

The Blackfriars was costing money, money out with none coming in. In the spring, if the Globe remained shut by Government edict, well, they might all start thinking of retirement as his friend Shakespeare already appeared to be doing. Old fears about going back into the grocery business narked at him. An old age sat in the corner of his wife's shop loomed alarmingly.

'Money?' he demanded.

'I think we can do better than *Richard*, in pounds, not shillings.'

Forty pounds was an awful lot of money.

'What's in it for you?' Hemmings demanded.

Palmer intended to take a cut of the money, four pounds, enough to keep body and soul together for the best part of a year.

'Salisbury will recompense me.'

Hemmings gave him one last, long look.

'I'll talk to the senior men about it. They may want to humour Middleton – we haven't so many writers that we shouldn't look after this one. A private reading? You guarantee it?'

Palmer knew he was home and dry. How could the actors resist?

Word came back to Palmer from Hemmings that the senior men were biddable. There was only one hurdle to cross, the co-author, Thomas Middleton. Palmer was unsure why – the King's Men had paid for the play, hadn't they? It was surely theirs to do with as they chose.

'It's a matter of what the French call etiquette,' Hemmings explained, 'the proper order of things. We like to keep our authors happy.'

He made the necessary introductions at the little alehouse near the Globe on Bankside.

Palmer had asked around about the playwright in advance: above thirty, or so he'd heard, a bricklayer-turned-gentleman's son, his gentility improved by going to the University at Oxford. An early career as an unsuccessful poet had forced him into political pamphleteering.

'One of them led to a Parliamentary enquiry,' the old official told him, 'but we feel,' which meant Whitehall felt, 'he calmed down as he went on. He has a line in city comedies, he is also close to the City of London Corporation – he puts on pageants for them. The City's judgement in these matters is usually sound and unimpeachable.'

The man Palmer met appeared suitably respectable and businesslike.

'My fee for the play has already been paid by the King's Men,' Middleton said.

Palmer was sure something extra could be found, by the acting company. They didn't need to, but he saw it as an extra inducement.

'I'm not at all sure that is the case.'

Hemmings's contradiction was bluster, Palmer felt sure and found a way of saying so.

'You and I know how generous the head fee will be,' he told him.

'If that is so,' Middleton gracefully conceded, 'what advantage is there to me, beyond the pecuniary? *Timon* has never been completed, never performed.'

'Exactly!' Palmer said. 'Now it will see the light of day.'

'In a private performance, in front of an audience of one?'

'An extremely influential one, the Chief Minister, after the King the greatest patron of our age.'

Middleton appeared unconvinced.

'What is the secret purpose here?' he said. 'If it is political, well, I have no interest. There have been times when I did – who among us writers hasn't?'

'Like Mr Jonson?' Palmer speculated.

Jonson was a bricklayer's stepson and proud of the trade. Palmer judged it wise not to assume the same about Thomas Middleton, Gentleman.

'I think you will find,' Middleton said, his upper lip lifting into a narrow smile, 'that Mr Ben Jonson will have no truck with me.'

'Thomas here took sides against Ben,' Hemmings confided to Palmer. 'Someone guyed Jonson in a play as a snake in the grass, Ben insulted him back, tit for tat in several more and other playwrights joined in.'

'The war of the theatres they called it,' – that narrow Middleton smile again – 'excellent publicity all round. But not conducive to friendship.'

'So *Timon* is to be a stillborn child,' Palmer said.

A furrow creased Middleton's forehead.

'One door closes, another opens,' the writer said. 'I'm not bound to any company, I have always been a free agent.'

'Thomas started out with Henslow and the Lord Admiral's Men,' Hemmings explained to Palmer. 'Prince Henry's Men as they are now.'

'I wrote for them, John, as I've written for you and for others. As for *Timon*, I imagine we might return to it some day?'

Palmer intervened.

'Not according to Mr Shakespeare. *Timon* is dead in his cave. His heart's not in it.'

Middleton looked enquiringly towards Hemmings.

'Well, that is *one* opinion ... and a very important one too. But Will isn't here, he's away in Stratford ... again. But he would admit that the play, unfinished as it stands, remains the property of our company. We could, for example, sell it to a publisher – there has been interest.'

'So the play is company property,' Palmer reminded them both, 'a saleable commodity and sold it will most likely be for many pounds fewer than I can get for you. As for Mr Shakespeare, he is not here and so he is unable to help us with his advice on this current opportunity.'

He watched Middleton carefully. The man appeared to be teetering on the edge. He gave him a final push.

'How sad that *Timon* is not to be taken from the page to the stage just once...'

'Salisbury *is* coming?'

The voice belonged to Hemmings, his voice anxious, calling down from the stage inside the Blackfriars playhouse.

The atmosphere was intimate, candlelight softening the winter light creeping in through high windows. The room was squarish, fitted out in dark woods, more like a chapel and so a world away from the hurly-burly of a vast open-air theatre.

The Chief Minister was late, by more than an hour.

Palmer consoled himself with the money for the players and playwright in one purse and his own reward – four handsome pounds – in another. He'd had more trouble with Salisbury's old official than with Middleton and Hemmings, over the size of the fee and its payment through him, but in the end he had prevailed.

A sound from behind alerted him.

He turned to see the old official, wringing his hands in unspoken apology for the late arrival. Beyond him was a man Palmer barely recognised. He had to look twice.

Salisbury, Robert Cecil that was, was a puckered wraith. He was moving slowly, all the juice sucked out of what had never been succulent flesh in the first place.

The tiny statesman straightened himself up. The constriction in his chest whistled in disharmony with the words he spoke, like an untuned squeezebox.

'Gentlemen,' he said, barely audible. 'I have waited long for this … privilege.'

He started to move painfully forwards, stopping to cough, a wracking cough. He walked to where Palmer was standing, ignoring his presence. His breathing was coming heavily. With effort, he sat down on a bench, placing both palms over the silver head of a cane relieved of his featherweight.

Palmer waved for the players to begin. A brief silence fell broken by the sound of actors entering.

Up on the stage, a quintet of chancers, their boots and shoes clattering on the wooden planks, compared what each had ready to offer rich Timon of Athens at exorbitant cost.

'Trumpets sound!'

The voice was Middleton's, reading from his manuscript.

The announcement jerked the little politician's head up, as if he knew it must signal the start of the main business of the play. Timon entered, Burbage uncostumed, taking up his habitual position centre-stage to say that this, this is the man you have all been waiting for.

'Burbage,' Palmer heard Salisbury wheeze, 'of course.'

Can a man act without the aid of costume, Palmer wondered? He was quickly answered.

Timon, not Burbage, relieved a friend's heavy debt. A reluctant father he persuaded to part with his daughter by matching her dowry. He gave poet, painter and jeweller custom or hope of it. His open-handedness was being made manifest.

Hemmings stepped forward, cast as a philosopher determined to tell home truths to power and wealth.

I come to have thee thrust me *out of doors!*

... for telling the rich man what was what.

He rounded on Timon's parasites for feeding on the rich man's generosity yet it was Timon who challenged him in return with a paean to the merits of friendship. Meantime the wheezing sound of Salisbury's infirmity distracted Palmer.

Middleton stood forward again.

'We omit here the masque of Cupid and the Amazons.'

Just as well, Palmer thought, whose buttocks had seized up once before at the masqueing game.

Timon ordered his steward to bring out a jewel cask, miming a gift of a precious stone to each of his departing guests. Gifts given to him he out-gave in ever-bigger gestures.

It provoked his steward.

His promises fly so beyond his state
That what he speaks is all in debt.

Palmer sensed Salisbury stir beside him. Wasn't this the politician's experience with the King, commanded to pay what could not be found? Catching the eye of the old official, Palmer was reassured that it was.

Timon's creditors crowded round him urgent in their demands – the word had gone round. His steward retreated, flooded by a mass miming of bills. Timon faced his humiliation with uncomprehending embarrassment.

'He will blame his steward.'

Salisbury was heard only by Palmer and his old official.

On cue onstage above, to his steward's home truths of accounts rendered but ignored, of property borrowed against or forfeited, of the costs of riotous entertainment, lights, music, Timon gave his answer – his friends! He would send to his friends, friends he had generously supported.

No doubt they would help him out by return.

One by one, all the lame, fair-weather excuses came back, why this one could not, or that one would not give back, not even in the tiniest part, what they had been given.

Timon ordered a last banquet.

'Dishes are uncovered and found to be full of water,' Middleton announced, reading from the stage directions. 'The water is thrown in the guests' faces.'

Timon's curses rained down on them too.

'The scene changes to outside the walls of Athens. My Lord,' Middleton began to say in Salisbury's direction, 'at this point I give way to the pen of my colleague Mr Shakespeare.'

Shakespeare's Timon ranted against the injustice of men.

Piety and fear
Religion to the gods, peace, justice, truth,
Domestic awe, night-rest, and neighbourhood,
Instruction, manners, mysteries, and trades,
Degrees, observances, customs and laws
Decline to your confounding contraries
And let confusion live.

The effect was like an old-style preacher hurling anathema to the four corners of the room. Even to Palmer's ears it was vintage Shakespeare. Salisbury's wheezing quieted.

Timon fled the crowd to seek sanctuary 'in woods and cave,' as Middleton described out loud.

Timon knelt down to dig for food, roots imagined to be buried in the ground. Instead his hands described discovery of a pot, his face a picture of surprised wonder, his gestures more and more extravagant when they showed that, inside, the pot was full of gold.

He mimed giving the gold away, to a passer-by, a disgraced exile from the city. It was the golden-boy Alcibiades leading soldiers on to conquer Athens which had shown the temerity to exile him for conduct unbecoming.

Last visits from the philosopher and his steward could not bring Timon back to reason. Was Salisbury moved by sight of the faithful steward ministering to a spendthrift? He showed no sign of it. Senators came from Athens to offer Timon the dictatorship of the city if he would defend it against Alcibiades.

He could not care, Timon announced three times, not if the city was sacked, its old men assaulted, its maidens raped.

Timon hath made his everlasting mansion
Upon the beached verge of the salt flood

He retired, 'to his cave', Middleton announced, to die.

'Drums roll' – Middleton's voice again one final time, signifying the end.

The actors lowered their play rolls. Eyes turned towards Salisbury, Palmer's included.

The little relic of a man, with difficulty, stood up. He limped to the edge of the stage, calling the performers forward.

'You are indeed the King's Men,' he told them. 'How thankful we must be that His Majesty lives among us to curb such follies as you have shown us here today.'

Really? Palmer's eye attempted to catch the old official's who quickly looked away.

Salisbury half-turned to go.

'Oh!' he said, as if he had forgotten something. 'See how Athens suffered under democracy and republic and how thankful we must be for monarchy.'

His audience dutifully laughed. Salisbury turned, with difficulty, to go.

Palmer was following the tiny body out of the playhouse when Salisbury paused. Without turning round to face Palmer he spoke.

'Go your way, Dick, go your way.'

Palmer missed the allusion. He watched the tiny figure leave, followed by the old official. They were both going off into another world, or so it seemed to him.

'What did all that mean?' Hemmings asked Palmer after he received the fee for the occasion.

Palmer had no idea.

'You will get your permission to reopen,' he said instead.

Falling plague numbers allowed a short season over Easter at the Blackfriars playhouse.

To the moan of 'it's not the Globe', Cuthbert Burbage gave a swift reply – charging prices six times the usual, the tiny theatre would make as much money, maybe more. And they would be back at the Globe soon afterwards for the regular summer season, with old *Macbeth* and not so old *Cymbeline* to start with.

There was no appetite to risk a second showing of *Timon* at Court. The leading men decided it would be unwise.

'It is not a dish to set before the King.'

Their instinct was confirmed by the new Master of the Revels, Buc.

'The word from on high' he told Hemmings, meaning Salisbury, 'is that on no account must *Timon* be performed, anywhere.'

'Then what's the play for the Blackfriars to be?'

Buc's answer, *The Alchemist* by Jonson, caused surprise among the actors.

'Will gives way to Ben,' more than one voice whispered.

News of the Jonson play at the Blackfriars put Shakespeare, in Stratford, on his mettle.

He finished off his latest play, with a winter title despite its coming summer launch and rode back down to London with it.

Heads shook among his fellow actors when rumours went round the company that an actor as statue-coming-to-life was to be the central effect. Hadn't Jonson already done that in his masques? Where was the call for machinery in it? Weren't they falling behind the latest in what the public demanded? Had Shakespeare lost his touch?

The cost of entry to the Blackfriars, minimum price sixpence was more than Palmer wanted to pay. A wait of a few weeks allowed his penny to be put to better service at *Macbeth* and then *Cymbeline* at the Globe. At both he saw the quack Simon Forman, without Emilia. Both times Forman attached himself to Palmer, rehearsing the same question.

'And what was the moral of that?'

Avoid Scotland or Wales, Palmer was tempted to answer – there be strange folk there.

A parting remark of Forman's detained him.

'Good-looking woman, Mrs Lanier, don't you find Mr Palmer?'

Palmer had found so to his cost, once, a long time ago.

Forman pushed his goat face closer.

'Did you halek with her, Mr Palmer?'

'Did I what?'

'Halek, make the two-backed beast?'

The man's breath was putrid. Palmer gave him no answer, walking away to find fresher air.

More theatrical than the plays was the continuing drama of poor Arbella Stuart.

'One almost feels sorry for her,' the old official told Palmer.' In the Tower she is threatening not to eat! Last time, with the elder Seymour it brought her close to death.'

How convenient for King James, Palmer thought.

'Whoever can have been behind such a mad scheme?' he asked instead.

The names mentioned meant nothing to him.

About the effect of the *Timon* play on the Chief Minister, the old official was true to form. He clammed up.

~ 21 ~

WHEN PALMER presented her with a small stack of complimentary copies of her book as published by Bonian, Emilia was as excited as a little girl. Once again she reeled off the names of the high and mighty on her list for gift copies.

'There is a purpose in all this,' she said, seeing the sceptical look on Palmer's face. 'You know the privilege my husband received from the King?'

The patent for the weighing of hay. How could he forget it? More to the point, how could he forget the money attached to it?

'It has never been paid, not in full, often not at all.'

That was often the trouble with Stuart largesse, it was like the water in the dishes in Timon's last banquet, unmaterial.

'If I can gain new friends with my book, well-placed friends, friends who have the ears of those whose hands can loosen royal purse-strings...'

Palmer admired her tenacity.

Another pair of hands was at work elsewhere opening Emilia's book.

John Hemmings saw.

'Yes, I'd heard about that,' he said to his old friend William Shakespeare. 'Not something I'd buy myself. The lady doth protest too much.'

Shakespeare smiled.

'Her argument may have more merits than her verse.'

'Do you think it will give any further annoyance to Southampton?'

Southampton had the ear of royalty, of bishops, of censors.

Shakespeare doubted that it would.

'It's really an old style of devotional poem to the Passion of our Lord. Not Southampton's taste or our market, wouldn't you say?'

'We're ready with your latest,' Hemmings replied, meaning his winter play. 'It's a charmer, Will, among your very best, I truly believe.'

This was rare from John Hemmings. Shakespeare smiled at the compliment.

'I have something else in the magical vein,' he said. 'You remember that tale brought back about one of the ships in the Virginia expedition?'

The expedition backed by none other than the Earl of Southampton.

'The one wrecked in the Bermudas?'

'Yes, wrecked by tempest. I shall magic their isle…'

Hemmings rubbed his hands. This was good news – Will, back to his very best!

Ben Jonson's best was not the public verdict on *Catiline*, presented at the Globe.

Palmer liked it, especially the long Ciceronian speeches, the ones which lost the crowd if their rumbling undercurrent of distraction was anything to go by. Classical inspiration thrived in the man, Palmer judged, who had a taste for such things. He was less impressed by the actors' costumes, togas worn carelessly over contemporary clothes – Inigo Jones would never have allowed it! But this was the public not the private theatre. Its audience was more easily fooled.

From a distance, Palmer saw Jonson arguing with passers by. He couldn't make out what he was saying. Those nearer to the author did.

'You're all jig-mad. You're only happy if there's a song and dance!'

The Winter's Tale gained a far better reception despite its summer staging. It was not to Palmer's taste, particularly when Chorus Time came on to bridge the first to the second part of the story.

Impute it not a crime … that I slide over fifteen years.

Fifteen years! To Palmer, this *was* criminal. Aristotle would never have stood for it!

Overhead the clouds of May chased tails across an azure sky. As if on cue the stage filled with a jolly feast-time country crowd gathered for a sheep-shearing festival. Leather jerkins jostled dirty-white fleeces. A dance of unlikely, out-of-place satyrs stomped to a playhouse jig.

Even Palmer laughed when a swindling cut-purse in a multi-coloured costume which shouted 'rogue' entertained both crowds, onstage and off. The clown, Robert Armin, was a clever actor, nimble and musical, subtler than the shocking colours he wore.

The king and queen of the may, a royal prince in disguise and his shepherdess were taught the folly of their hopes when the prince's father, likewise disguised, denounced them. No romance for royal scions, then. Hadn't Lady Arbella Stuart just found that out for herself? And for the second time? The text was nothing if not topical.

How would it end?

A statue of the long-dead queen was revealed at the back of the stage below the gallery. Her drapes were royal purple, her crown a solid brassy gold which caught the summer light.

The crowd hushed, fascinated – the face and arms were painted warm, too warm in tone for real. Was the statue made of marble or plainer stone? Or painted wood perhaps?

The statue moved! The queen came to life!

She held out her hand to her husband and to her long-lost daughter – the shepherdess of course, re-made princess. From there it was a race to the closing jig.

The ubiquitous Forman stood in his way on Palmer's way out.

'No, *you* tell me the moral,' Palmer said before the quack could ask him.

'Do not trust dissimulators,' Forman pronounced, 'those who pretend to be what they are not.'

Palmer gave him a long, hard look.

Full fathom five thy fa...

The pen, moving over the parchment, was stopped mid-scratch by a knock at the penthouse door.

'There's a woman here to see you,' a voice called in from outside.

Shakespeare put his pen down, annoyed. He was behind on his Bermudas play which Buc, the new Master of the Revels wanted to see in manuscript before the private reading, unlike his predecessor. Might too much learning among the censors become a dangerous thing?

Had he time for a visitor?

The door opened. It took a moment or two for him to recognise the figure it revealed. It was Emilia Lanier.

'Have I disturbed you?' she asked, looking across at his writing.

He waved a noncommittal hand.

'We authors,' he joked, motioning her to another stool in the confined space.

'You have read my work?' she asked him as she sat down.

She did not ask him what he thought of it.

'You sound the trumpet for your sex,' he said, settling for a positive.

'Not stridently, I hope.'

'Do your noble patronesses approve?'

'I can't say. Living in exile from my lady, I see so little of them. We inhabit different worlds. Mine is on a lower plane.'

Shakespeare knew something of that. His own days as house poet to the young Lord Southampton had taught him as much – about his young lord's world, touching it but never truly a part of it. Thank God he'd chosen the public stage and its rewards. He was a man of substance in his own right, not a dweller in someone else's house.

'Are you and Lanier together?'

'We are. We have the boy.'

The word pricked him. It brought up the memory of his dead son. He would have been a grown man by now, likely married and with children and living the life of a gentleman in Stratford as his own father had intended for him, until the bad times came.

A second thought struck a sourer note, a suggestion once made slyly by the Palmer man, that Emilia's child was not the old Lord Chamberlain's (everyone knew that), not Southampton's either, but his, one of her three bedmates in a sonnet spring.

It didn't bear thinking about.

'How old is he?' he asked.

'Nineteen. He's a musician, aiming at the Court like many in my family have done before him. He is doing well.'

Shakespeare knew plenty of Bassanos and Laniers among the Court musicians. Musicians he liked, but not so much to want to adopt one as his son with all the complications it would bring at home in Stratford. A man looking at fifty could not know how many more years he might have. Exhausting them with Emilia, her and her unrelenting ambition, did not bear thinking.

'And you?' he asked her.

'I have my book. Lanier believes we will finally be paid for the patent he was granted by the King, this year or next.'

The King, when he paid, paid well, that much Shakespeare knew who never had to depend on it, unlike the woman in front of him.

'What can I do for you, Emilia?'

Did she really want him to acknowledge the boy? Unlikely, with Lanier around and, anyway, her dreams preferred the noble seed she habitually liked to claim for the boy's paternity. What substance was there for the child of a vagabond actor?

'I saw your play, the winter play.'

'Did you like it?'

She did not say why at first, or not in so many words, until:

'The scene of the statue coming to life … it was beautiful.'

A silence fell between them.

Did she think … did she really think … that he wrote it for her?

'I should like to have played that queen, in your statue scene.'

'If women publish books, perhaps one day we shall see them act on the stage,' he said in a light attempt at pleasantry.

'Do you think so?'

'Not in my time,' he said, meaning both their time. 'The Master of the Revels would have a fit, our licence would be revoked, our patent called in…'

'You have come a long way, Master Shakespeare,' she said.

It reminded him of the days before the coat of arms and his place with the King, the time when he had known her best and yet, not at all.

'We both have, Emilia,' he said.

~ 22 ~

N OW my charms are all o'erthrown...

The master-magician of the enchanted island stood centre-stage, begging his release from his audience, seeking their applause. There were no ambitious stage effects. Burbage as Prospero was illuminated by simple candelabras held in the hand of every actor standing around him.

He held out his broken staff.

It was the first night of the Christmas season at Court. The tale of shipwreck into a land of airy sprites and clumsy monsters, of love met by chance (or was it by design?), of justice done and revenge set aside pleased the onlookers without their fully understanding why.

The Great Chamber of the Palace was nearly cleared when Shakespeare wandered through.

'A mystery rather than a morality play?'

The voice stopped him in his tracks. It was Lord Southampton's.

Shakespeare turned to face it.

'I never know until it's performed,' he began to say. 'On the page it's words waiting for the alchemy of the stage to change it into gold; or it finds itself unchanged – poor, dull lead.'

'It was gold tonight.'

'Did it please its audience?'

'You heard the applause. Some say it's your farewell.'

Shakespeare laughed at the thought.

'Shades of the vanity of a poet and his sonnets? Look at *me*, look *at* me, *look* at me. I have no doubt that it was Prospero's farewell. Did Their Majesties enjoy it?'

Southampton thought of the Queen – yes, she did. As for the King, he was too busy ogling Robbie Carr, his latest puppy.

'Does it matter?'

'I am a King's Man. And so are you, my Lord.'

Yes he was, Southampton privately agreed. More prominent in the Court of the Queen, as it happened; but since this kept Her Majesty entertained and His Majesty free for his bosom friends, for his latest David or Jonathan, then yes, he was the King's man too.

'What's next?' he asked, the old, polite question.

Shakespeare laughed.

'Signatures for money taken, bills of sale and mortgages.'

Southampton waved such vulgar things aside.

'Must Prospero always come back for the jig?' Shakespeare asked.

Richard Bonian the publisher was perplexed at the sight of a woman standing before him.

'I am Mrs Lanier, wife of Captain Lanier, servant to the King.'

Bonian looked her up and down, sniffing trouble. She was, he quickly recognised from the name, one of his authors and authors could be trouble, usually before publication, sometimes after. It was usually to do with errors in the text and impossible demands for correction and re-publication. He steeled himself for the necessary, unnecessary argument.

'How may I help you?' he asked cautiously.

'I have come about my book.'

Bonian did not answer, waiting for her complaint. It didn't come.

'I am used to dealing with Mr Palmer about it,' Bonian said.

Emilia gave a slight movement of impatience.

'I am the author,' she said. 'Mr Palmer has done his job, there is nothing more for him to do.'

Certainly nothing she was prepared to pay him for.

'... I want to discuss the preparation of a special copy, for a special presentation.'

Bonian relaxed. This was easier, especially if the author was bound to pay. His eyes asked the question – presented, who to?

Emilia drew herself up to her full height.

'My Lady Cumberland...'

Fine, Bonian thought, it was perfectly normal to employ a noble dedicatee, even a female one.

'... my noble *friend*,' Emilia emphasised, 'has had indications that a wish would be favourably received of a gift to His Royal Highness...'

HRH! Which one, Bonian wondered?

'... His Royal Highness Prince Henry, Prince of Wales!'

Bonian was impressed. He gave a deft bow of willingness.

'It will be a matter for my printer Mr Sims, but you may by all means discuss it with me.'

He did not imagine the woman going in among the printing presses, the sweaty bodies and the ink-blackened hands and nails. Few authors did.

Emilia rehearsed what she had in mind.

'I shall want the best vellum, gilt-edged, leather covers....'

'The usual quarto size?'

'Yes, so that His Highness might easily carry it on his person.'

'And a new dedication to him, to be printed at the front?'

Emilia smiled at this, a knowing smile.

'We shall be discreet. Our advice,' from a royal source she hinted, 'says not, only that His Royal Highness's coat of arms should appear on the covers.'

'The ostrich feathers, gilded?'

What else, Emilia seemed to say before she spoke again.

'There are certain dedications from the existing text which will need ... ah...'

'Deleting?'

'Releasing.'

Both understood who, the unfortunate Lady Arbella who had offended her own royal family with her marriage antics. Arbella out, Henry in, in more senses than one.

'Now to terms, missus,' he said, having agreed her instructions.

One of Emilia's dark eyebrows shot up. Terms?

Bonian began to feel unusually anxious.

'What you propose that we prepare is costly, especially as a single item.'

Every writer should be forced into the printing works, to Bonian's mind to see what it took to set up the presses and in this case for a single copy. The time and effort cost money, in itself and in other work set aside. And it would require special supervision, in the typesetting and the proofing, given its royal destination.

'... the cost of the materials, the gilding, the paper and the leather covers are the very least of it.'

Emilia allowed the question to float between them before speaking out in her lady-in-waiting-to-nobility voice.

'Master Bonian, we are talking of a gift to the Heir to the Throne of England. Have your works,' and here her voice shifted down in tone to the insinuating, 'ever been given to a future King?'

'No, but...'

Bonian began to sense the ground shifting under his feet. He took a mental quarter off the price, he halved it. Looking back at Emilia Lanier, he saw that it would do him no good. The thought of his book in the hands of the Prince began to take over. It could do no harm, it could do him good.

'What if,' he began to say before his courage nearly failed him, 'what if we produce it gratis?'

Richard Palmer had a plan of his own. His target was George Wilkins.

He started low, with the official Aletaster in Clerkenwell.

'So you're sayin' 'e waters 'is beer?'

Which landlord didn't in the dens of thieves, whores and pickpockets busy in the mazy streets off Smithfield Market? The difference was, this was a formal complaint, and a formal complaint was something for an officer to 'act upon', and this officer liked 'acting upon'. A man who 'acted upon' got promoted, to Constable or maybe better.

Palmer had judged his man well.

When the Aletaster went into Wilkins's tavern to do what his title described a rumpus broke out, right enough, which justified the ring of stout men he had made sure to come protected by.

'This 'ere beer's not up to strength!'

... which was when the trouble kicked off.

As the Aletaster backed out of the tavern surrounded by his defenders, he launched a parting shot.

'You'll be 'earin' from us, Master Wilkins, just you see if you doesn't!'

Palmer's next conversation, with the Constable, was less clearcut.

A man who had arrived in the Constable's high position was careful what he 'acted upon', preferring, wherever possible, not to 'act upon' anything at all.

'If I arrested everyone what keeps a bawdy house, or an establishment frequented by lewd women, as you puts it, I should be busy day and night and all year round!'

'There's no need to arrest him,' Palmer said.

The answer soothed the Constable who liked to be known as 'Uncle', one who fixed things so that they ran smoothly without involving the courts. He liked the sound, and safety of 'no arrests'.

'What do you suggest?' he asked, heartened that Palmer was a man after his own.

Why go locking people up after all? What good did it do?

'What if Wilkins is going up in front of the Justices anyway?'

'What for?'

'For watering his beer. What if the charge is that he is not a fit person?'

'A fit person for what?'

The Constable's eyes widened as he caught the drift.

'... I *see*, not a fit person to hold his licence.'

But why should he help, the Constable asked himself?

Trouble came regularly to Wilkins's tavern, caused often as not by the landlord himself. The Constable didn't like trouble, he tried to avoid it as much as possible but the trouble in Wilkins's establishment, it just kept on coming back. People were saying that the Aletaster, a stouter heart in *their* opinion, was after his job. Remove Wilkins, close down his tavern, problem solved *and* a mark tallied up in his, the Constable's favour.

He couldn't let his rival the Aletaster take the credit, could he?

If enough officers gave evidence in front of the Justices…

The day Wilkins appeared in court, Palmer made a point of being there before him. One of the presiding Justices, he saw, was large and fat; the other was slight and thin.

'We call him the radish, two long, thin legs and a tiny body,' the Clerk of the Court confided to Palmer while his palm was being greased. 'He's your man, he tells the other one what to think.'

Wilkins was called. He did not look happy. When he cast his eye round the court, Palmer gave him an encouraging smile. Wilkins's eyes narrowed.

The Constable read out the case against him.

'What have you to say?' the fat Justice demanded, prompted by the thin one.

Wilkins's chest inflated, as if to blow away the Aletaster, the Constable and the whole damned lot of them! Then he looked across at Palmer.

It was time to change his story – the Aletaster had evidence after all.

'I accept the charge about the beer. The fault was not mine, it was in the brewing which was done elsewhere, that is, by others.'

A likely story.

'... as for lewd women, I do my best to keep them out, as the court well knows.'

He had been summoned before for violence towards one. On the other hand, he had helped another escape who was being pursued for theft.

The two Justices whispered among themselves. The fat one spoke.

'As you admit yourself, Master Wilkins, you have been before this court before and its patience with you is *out*! We order the removal of your licence until you can prove that you are once again a fit person to hold it.'

Wilkins made to speak out. Instead he stopped and scowled, at the bench and then at Palmer. For a moment they stared each other out before Wilkins turned on his heel and stomped out.

Rot in hell on earth, Palmer wished his departing back. This is the beginning of your end.

He judged it wise to absent himself from Clerkenwell for the time being. Why not make a holiday of it? He withdrew some savings from the Cheapside goldsmith and travelled with a carrier's party in the direction of Oxford.

They were joined at the last minute by a gentleman. Palmer recognised Sir George Buc at once. He kept his distance from him. So it surprised him when, with Tyburn and it gibbets behind them and the road to Oxford lying open ahead, Buc spurred his horse forward towards him.

'What takes you away from London?' Buc asked him, too affably for Palmer's taste from one who'd had him dismissed him from office.

'I might ask you the same, sir.'

'A visit to one of the colleges,' Buc said, 'to look over some old books.'

... on his obsession, the last Plantagenet, Richard III, a king his ancestors had loyally followed; the topic was safer under the Stuarts than it had ever been under the Richard-killing Tudors.

'... and you?'

'I travel to see a family I know, and my god-daughter.'

'Would I know them?'

'I doubt it, sir. They keep the Crown Tavern.'

Buc laughed, more frankly this time.

'The Davenants? I know them, from their time in London. In fact I shall be staying with them as well. One needs protection from the dons in your Oxford colleges, wouldn't you agree?'

Palmer said he would. He was a Cambridge man.

They rode on a little further without speaking.

'So you are little Miracle's godfather?' Buc said.

Palmer was staggered, too staggered to confirm or deny.

'I know the story,' Buc said, 'but I never knew your name. The Davenants have always been guarded about it.'

Good for them, Palmer thought. Did they know Buc's position? Palmer had never mentioned him by name and which gentleman explained himself to a tavern-keeper?

'... but not little Miracle, however. *She* is very indiscreet. So I knew *a* name, which wasn't much help – Uncle Two-Names. Am I right?'

Palmer turned an honest face towards the Master of the Revels and nodded.

'Yes, it made their Good Samaritan sound even more mysterious,' Buc said.

The day was fine, the first of the year when the heat of the sun was settling on the ground without reduction from wind or cloud. The buzzing of insects, signifying busyness sounded like the noises of sleep. Palmer began to doze on horseback.

'It was Tilney wanted you out,' Buc disturbed him by saying, 'may he rest in peace.'

Did Palmer believe him?

'... he said you were Salisbury's spy. Were you?'

He had been, Palmer admitted to himself.

'Not for some years,' he said.

'Never again, I think, Mr Palmer. Haven't you heard the news? Lord Salisbury is dead, on the road back from a cure in Bath.'

Salisbury, Robert Cecil, *dead*?

The news reduced Palmer to silent thought.

An image crept into his mind, not of the man in office, in his office plotting, weaving, writing, holding all the reins of State in hand or calling down retribution on traitors in the halls of justice. It was an image instead of a slight, misshapen youth in a Cambridge college, second son of a famous father, of whom little was expected.

'I shall be too busy to see much of you in Oxford,' Buc said.

He bet he would, Palmer reckoned, brought back to the reality of the day – the 'how good to see you and goodbye'.

'... but when you are back in London, come and see me. There's too much work these days in the office of the Revels.'

Buc spurred his horse forwards.

Palmer watched him go, the hooves of the trotting horse raising little puffs of dust. The day, the year, his life appeared to be taking on a brighter colour.

Then the old truculence set in. When his horse tried to follow Buc's, Palmer reined it back.

~ Closing the File ~

'YER'VE ONLY GOT yerself to blame.'

The voice was the landlord's, in the Bell Inn, Carter Lane hard by St Paul's Cathedral.

Palmer shrugged.

He had decided not to go back into the censor's employment. It had been Salisbury's idea and Salisbury was dead – the governing intelligence in the State was no more.

Gone too was a shinier star, the State's great hope for the future.

The Heir to the Throne, Prince Henry was dead at eighteen, from drinking in foul water while out swimming in the Thames. A fever had done for the lad.

So many hopes went down with him, Emilia's among them if it was true what Palmer had heard, a story the publisher Bonian was telling against himself, about how she had talked him into a presentation copy of her book to the Heir Apparent. More Unapparent now...

Lady Arbella, Prince Henry, it would be a wise potentate who avoided Emilia's next offer of a dedication.

As for the great matter of the royal succession, there was at least a spare. The next in line was a tiny brother, Charles. The name had no precedent among English princes. It was not, Palmer thought, a good omen albeit the Stuart grip on the Throne appeared settled.

'I've got news for you,' the landlord added.

Palmer raised his eyes from his pint pot. His credit ought still to be good.

'Happened this afternoon. That playhouse of yours – the Globe...'

Hardly his, the actors', William Shakespeare's.

'What of it?'

'It's burned down. I 'ad it on good authority – one of the watermen as plies his craft over to Bankside, 'e drinks here. Ses they was playing some play 'bout good old 'Enery Six-Wives.'

Palmer sat up straight on his stool.

'How did it happen?'

Why didn't he know?

'Looks like they was lettin' off some cannon, blank-shot like, just the waddin' in the barrel, to salute the play-king. Well, it caught in the thatch o' the roof and set fire to it. I always says, tiles is safer than thatch...'

'Many dead?' Palmer asked.

Fire in London was a killer.

'That's what's odd about it – none. Oh, there was one had his breeches set on fire. They put it out with a flagon of ale.'

What a waste of beer, the eyes of each man said to the other.

'In the midst of life we are in death,' Palmer half-remembered from the book of prayer, or was it from the new Bible King James had caused to be published a year or two ago, scoring points against his adversaries on both sides of religion, high and low?

Another death had recently been reported to him. Widow Lanier was now Emilia's title. Her bully boy husband, the ex Court musician turned soldier of fortune, Lanier the broken-nosed, broken by Palmer himself, was dead, cause not given.

What would she do now, he asked himself, cheated of royal patronage, bereft of her great ladies, robbed of a husband, more to the point, of his Government sinecure unless she could make a claim to have inherited it? How old was her boy the musician? More than twenty, Palmer estimated. She'd have some support from him, he supposed but it was a world away from the glorious ambitions of her youth.

Palmer too would have to make his own way. His friend the old official had gone into retirement somewhere unknown after the death of his master. Even the quack Forman was reported dead despite all his nostrums for good health. Could a man die from halitosis? Ben Jonson now, he was still going strong. Shakespeare? Rarely seen in London these days. Would the fire at the Globe keep him away or bring him hurrying back?

As for business, Palmer was running out of imagination. His reports to the old Alderman about his wife, thrusting arse and spreading thighs just didn't do it any more. He ought to be worried. He couldn't bring himself to be so.

This year was his fiftieth. Palmer raised his mug in salutation to ghosts remembered and forgotten. The landlord saw it. He called for more beer.

www.ingramcontent.com/pod-product-compliance
Lightning Source LLC
Chambersburg PA
CBHW020941180626
46814CB00003B/896